Callihan: Valley of Skulls

Callihan: Valley of Skulls

Callihan
Book 1

L.J. Martin

WISE WOLF
BOOKS

Author's Note

Although a work of fiction actual history and historical figures are portrayed in the Callihan series. Day to day conversations may be fictionalized but no portrayal of actual characters and their actions, either positive or negative, is written unless gleaned from good historical sources or of no consequence. The Earps and Doc Holliday will play major roles in the next Callihan novel, titled *Callihan: The Earps*.

Callihan: Valley of Skulls

Chapter One

If I'd have reached for a star and drew my hand back to find a fist full of diamonds, I wouldn't have been more surprised than I was when she returned my smile and howdy with a "Good morning" just outside of Taggart's Merchandise that cold December Saturday, the year of our Lord 1879.

I did not consider myself appealing to the ladies and my most aggressive approach to women folk was to snatch my hat off and lower my eyes with a nod when a lady passed. I guess I was a bit hypnotized by Sarah Ann's beauty, so much so I couldn't take my eyes off'n her, thus my eye contact and schoolboy grin that morn. I later learned she was nearing her eighteenth birthday and me six months past my nineteenth, her just returned from Boston and a fine education and me just finished a four-year stint as a smithy's apprentice but now the proud owner of Fenton's Forge, as Buck Fenton's heart had failed him and I was the only friend the growling and snapping old bear of a man had in the world. Thus, I'd been the only name in his will. Even being an independent businessman didn't seem to make me fittin' for Sarah Ann in her daddy's steely gaze.

It was two months to gain her daddy's trust so I could come calling and another month a'fore he'd let us perch ourselves on the bench just outside the front door of the Bar Five ranch house occupied by Sarah Ann, her ma and pa, and her four brothers...three older, one younger. Smithy was an honorable trade in most eyes but Mr. Seth MacIntosh, who ran several thousand cattle—even he didn't know how many—and over five hundred head of horses, thought the black-smith trade a lowly occupation, even below the two dozen cowhands he employed. I cared little what he thought but acted as if he was at the right hand of God to please my sainted hoped-for future wife.

It was near a year before the old man consented to our nuptials—as I understood that only due to the badgering of Mrs. MacIntosh—and only another week before he banned me from ever stepping foot near the Bar Five again.

That only moments after we threw the first shovel full of dirt on Sarah Ann Macintosh Donahey's coffin.

Mr. MacIntosh eyed me with a look that would melt a horseshoe. "I'd damn sure kill you where you stand had my daughter not loved you so. But should you ever step within .44-40 range of my home again, I'll set her feelings aside and it'll be your face getting a shovel full." With that and a glare from each of her brothers, and a sad smile and shake of the head from her mother, that they all gave me their back and walked away following the near hundred ranch and town folks who'd attended Sarah Ann's funeral.

Fact is it was Sarah Ann's wanting to distance herself from the iron hand of her pa and vigilance of her older brothers that got her killed and cost me a gouge, now a scab, across the back of my neck. A half inch nearer my spine and it would have likely killed us both.

Had I not been angry to the marrow and hungry to revenge her, I wished it had killed me.

Who fired that fateful shot and his demise, as

painful as I can conjure it, will here-to-fore be my life's work.

As it was Sarah Ann's wish I'd sold the forge, concluding the transaction just a day before our wedding and it was aboard the Concord stage to Wickenburg following that five masked robbers had stopped the stage with a fallen ponderosa not a quarter mile short of Iron Springs. When Toby Willard, who was riding shotgun, swung on them, they opened fire, at least two heavy slugs knocking him out of his seat to the rocks near the two-track road. The shot that killed Sarah Ann, striking her just below the left ear, creased me on the back of my neck and dizzied me so badly I couldn't focus my gaze on my instantly dead bride. We were dragged out of the coach and dropped in the dust—one of them jerking my revolver from its holster—as the bandits beat the other two passengers senseless with rifle butts. They dropped the strongbox from behind the legs of Oscar Aldridge, the whip, after mounting the coach across the boot and beating Oscar, crushing his skull with the butt of a heavy revolver.

All this I observed as if looking through a storm cloud and feeling like I'd been struck by a bolt of lightning, even my hearing seemed as if those talking were deep in a mine and voices echoed over each other.

It was a blessed moment when I passed out, only to wake sometime later—no idea how long—to find myself the only soul alive. Oscar, the whip; Toby, the shotgun guard; a fella named Augustus, "call me Gus" who claimed agricultural implement drummer; and a Spaniard who'd introduced himself as Don Emilio Bustamante, were all dead. But it was not them that caused my eyes to fill with tears, my heart to near stop, my breathing to catch until my lungs cried out for even the dry hot air. The only grace to Sarah Ann's death was she was struck before we even knew we were being robbed. Hopefully before any fear flooded her. Still dizzy, my head throbbing, my chest heaving, and my eyes flooded with tears, I sat legs outstretched and lifted her bloody head to my lap.

And cried.

Charley Wong, the Bar Five cook had driven us from the ranch after the wedding and the Macintoshes filling nearly one hundred guests full of beer, whiskey, and a half beef turned over an open fire, in time to catch a four o'clock Concord from the station in Prescott to Wickenburg.

It was our plan to survey until we found the

right place to use the proceeds of the sale of Fenton's Forge to establish another like establishment wherever looked to be the most promising, even if it meant prospecting all the way to California. And Sarah Ann brought a two-thousand-five-hundred-dollar dowry which was to be used to buy and furnish a fine house. It, and the one thousand two hundred dollars of the proceeds of the sale of Fenton's Forge, were now mostly in the filthy hands of five thieves.

I've never considered myself a particularly cautious soul, however, it has long been my habit when traveling to line my brogans with paper money and my wide leather belt was handmade with pockets on the inside and held eight twenty-dollar gold eagles. Them and the paper money in my brogans meant I was left with five hundred which was enough for a good horse, bedroll, bridle, saddle, shotgun, 73 Winchester, and Colt revolver. And plenty of ammunition.

We had yet to have a quiet moment in a fine hotel room to consummate our marriage.

I've never considered myself a violent man. I've never thought vengeance or retribution truly an answer to any of man's misdeeds. I've been taught forgiveness the road to one's own peace of mind and salvation.

To hell with that.

Vengeance now eats at my guts as if a ravenous snake is coiled there, and I fear will until I have five heads—likely more—on stakes, eyes bulging and being picked by crows, distended tongues being scorched by the burning sun.

My life's work has taken a new direction.

Chapter Two

My pa, Ian Donahey, brought us to Prescott at the conclusion of the War of Rebellion, as many south of the Mason Dixon line called the affair. Being born in 1860 I was hardly aware of the fighting. Prescott had just been designated the Capital of the Arizona Territory, replacing Fort Whipple, but the capital was soon moved to Tucson, then back to Prescott in 1877. Pa was a cooper and wheelwright and served in the Union, thank God normally well behind the lines, repairing the wagons that kept Mr. Lincoln's army on the move.

Ma, Mildred, was a fine Christian woman, the fourth of eleven children sired by my grandma and grandpa Murphy who immigrated from

County Cork in Ireland. Which is why I began life with the handle Conn Murphy Donahey.

It pains me to report my folks both passed of the Cholera when I was but fifteen. Our cabin and five acres just northwest of town was sold to satisfy Pa's debts and I consigned myself to old man Fenton and the life of a smithy. My younger siblings, sister Fiona and brother Hugh were sent to St. Louis to live with my uncle and aunt. At fifteen I was near six feet tall and after helping Pa with wheels and hogshead barrels, many over one hundred pounds, I was stout. In fact, I impressed many by being able to bend a horseshoe without the aid of a hammer. After four years with Fenton pounding iron and leaning on stock to lift strong legs to be shod there were few men who wanted to test my mettle with a wrestle or weight lift.

A horse backer, traveling west, came along not long after I'd cradled Sarah Ann's head in my lap. He easily jumped the fallen log and alarmed the small trading post at Iron Springs which dispatched a couple of fellas with axes and cross-cuts. Soon their flatbed farm wagon could pass. They loaded me, Sarah Ann, and the drover side by side in the wagon bed and lit out for Prescott.

I'd known Doc Boynton for many years. He took charge of Sarah Ann's body, to my dismay as

I foolishly wanted to keep holding her hand. After quieting me with a large dose of laudanum he sent me on to the hospital at nearby Fort Whipple, where I awoke to see an Army orderly reading a month's old Leslie's Weekly. I cleared my throat, which sent a bolt of pain through my hard head, and he looked over the paper and announced, "The doc will want to know you're awake."

Not only the doc returned with the orderly but Seth MacIntosh and his oldest son Rafe stomped along close behind. Even before the doc could examine me, he was shoved aside and Seth hunkered over me, hands on hips, jaw tight. He eyed me up and down before speaking.

"You don't look so damned injured to me. How is it you let my daughter die?"

I tried to clear my thinking before answering. "Shot came out of nowhere. Creased the back of my neck...and seems to me, same bullet hit Sarah Ann."

"Humph," he snorted. "You was healed, wasn't ya?"

"I was."

"Then why the hell didn't you shoot it out with them no-accounts?"

"The driver yelled down there was a tree down

across the road and had just reined up when I was hit—"

"Hell's fire, you are barely grazed."

"Shot knocked me silly. I could barely see or hear. I passed out—"

"Worthless as tits on a boar. I told Sarah Ann time and time again you was worthless. Strong arm don't mean a piddlin' amount of brain or good sense. Worthless, no education, no—"

The doctor interrupted him. "You'll leave now, Mr. Macintosh. No matter what you think, this boy is hurt. Leave, now!"

"Worthless as a sterile bull—"

The doc cleared his throat as he stepped between Seth and the bed. He jammed a stiff finger into Seth's deep chest. "You take a whack on your Atlas and see how you do."

"Atlas?"

"The spine nearest your skull. It's amazing this boy is alive."

"Ha, it'll be amazing if'n he lives long." Seth spun on his heel but his boy Rafe, a hulking sort with deep-set eyes and the brow of an angry circus gorilla, leaned over and glared at me.

"Sarah Ann's dying is on you, Donahey. You ain't seen the end of this."

I didn't respond.

The old man paused at the doorway and yelled back. "You owe me twenty-five hundred dollars. You can take it to the Stockman's Bank. I don't want to see you near the Bar Five."

I didn't bother to mention Sarah Ann's dowry went with my money and the strong box...the robbers bounty.

I didn't see the Macintosh family for three days until they buried her in Prescott's Pioneer Cemetery.

It was against the doc's wishes I'd dressed and headed to the funeral and it was obvious as a wart on the end of your nose I was unwelcome. I stayed well back and stood, hat in hand, until all had left the grounds and only then walked over and kneeled while two Mexicans backfilled her grave. They ignored me and kept working while I spoke loud enough for any to hear.

"Darling, if it helps you rest easy, go on to sit at the right hand of God knowing them who sent you on your way will die a hard death before they rot in hell. I swear that, as God is my witness."

I readjusted my hat and headed out to Goldwater's Mercantile to stock up on all I figured I'd need for a long quest. In addition to the belly gun I kept in my boot, unfound by the bandits, I was soon in possession of a fine 73 Winchester and

Colt revolver, both in .44-40; a double twelve-gauge short-barreled coach gun; a bedroll and canteen, and the simple accoutrements to camp in mountains or desert. From there, I moved across the plaza to Alleandro's Hostelry. Alleandro de Zugasti was known to sell the finest horses and tack in Yavapai County. And I hoped the fifteen and a half hand dappled gray gelding I bought was as fine as Alleandro professed as I laid out seventy-five dollars for him and a saddle with tall forks, horn, and cantle. He threw in deep saddlebags, and I paid another six dollars for saddle scabbards for the long arms and a saddle holster for the Colt.

The hell of it was I had seldom had the need of a firearm other than the small caliber single shot Pa assigned me along with the task of bringing in squirrel, rabbit, quail or turkey. I was no shootist or quick draw gunfighter...but I meant to rectify that.

I knew, very slightly, two fellas in Prescott who were renowned for their ability to face down malcontents and I meant to have one of them teach me the use of the sidearm in challenging situations.

Heading for the new Palace Saloon I meant to employ either Mr. Virgil Earp, who was a Prescott deputy marshal; him or a gentleman gambler who went by the handle Doc—reputed to have been a dentist at times past—to teach me proficiency. I'd need some skills if I was to finish my task. I'd had some brief conversations with both men, having shod horses for them, but the extent of those exchanges were me saying "four bits" unless a new shoe was required then "six bits" and them giving me a nod and later an "obliged" or "thanks."

So, I knew them by sight and sordid stories of their accomplishments.

I tied the gray at the rail outside and pushed thru the batwings. The bartender, Alexis Towbridge, was a friend of sorts as I'd played dominos with him at a table in the square on more than one Sunday afternoon.

I approached him as my eyes adjusted to the dim light and climbed up on a barstool. He wiped the bar with a towel as he came my way.

"By all that's holy if it ain't Conn Donahey. I don't believe you've ever graced the Palace. What's your pleasure?"

Alexis was not a pleasant fellow to look upon as he'd been cursed with the smallpox at some time past. He was pocked more than the surface of the moon and to add insult to that injury he'd had a run-in with the Apache and a nearly round four inches of scalp on his pate was now scarred. If anyone should have never removed their hat, it was Alexis. I'd oft times wondered if he hadn't been hired to scare the customers into good behavior.

"I would enjoy a beer, sir," I replied, fishing a dime out of my pocket and slapping it on the bar. "And some guidance..."

"Where is it you'd like to go?" he asked as he pulled a mug of Excelsior ale.

"Not a where but a who."

"So, who?" He placed the beer before me and snatched up the dime.

"Deputy Marshal Virgil Earp or Doc Holliday?"

Chapter Three

"Earp works the evenings doing his rounds and will stick his head in..." He pulled his pocket watch from a waistcoat pocket, "it's three, so in four or five hours as he makes his rounds. Holliday is in the back skinning a couple of drovers out of their hard-earned at the faro table."

I toasted him with the mug. "Obliged." And headed to the back.

I sidled up to a table near the back entrance and stood behind two seated fellas in floppy brimmed hats and dusters and another with a bowler, city suit, and eyeglasses round as a twenty-dollar gold piece.

Holliday was not one to miss much so I wasn't

surprised when he didn't even bother to look up but addressed me as he dealt.

"Howdy, Smithy. You come to try your luck or just stand there like a bumpkin. There's a seat open and I believe it's the lucky one."

I couldn't help but smile as he seemed the expert at getting folks to join the game. I did not take the seat but rather answered, "Mr. Holliday, I believe I'll save my money as I need someone with your skills to give me some lessons for which I'll pay a dollar an hour."

"Younger, I wouldn't walk across to the square and beat you at horseshoes for a dollar an hour."

"Then two, and the time can be at your pleasure, so long as it's soon."

He stopped dealing and looked up for the first time. "And this lesson is?"

"I am the owner of a new Colt and would like to become proficient with it."

"And your reason for these lessons?"

"Some no accounts killed my wife of six hours and justice calls."

He eyed me for a long moment. "I heard about that incident out near Iron Springs, correct?"

"Yes, sir."

"Probably something you should leave to the law, son," he said, and went back to dealing. I was a little taken aback by his calling me "son" as he appeared only ten years or so older. The rumor was he was riddled with consumption and had come west for the dry air to heal himself. He was nearly or as tall as myself but thin, so much as to appear a little gaunt. He did sport a fine mustache which filled out his face somewhat.

I cleared my throat so my voice would have some conviction. "Well, sir, you might be right. But that wouldn't give me the pleasure of seeing that murderous scum meet their maker. I'm going after them if I have to do it with a dinner fork or my bare hands."

He chuckled at that, then stopped dealing and looked up again. "I'd hate to see a young fella shot full of holes before..." He had to cough a gob of spit up and mop his mouth with a rag before continuing. "...before he could get iron in hand, so's I'm your huckleberry. You meet me in the early afternoon, tomorrow, say two o'clock, behind Quinton's Livery and bring a bottle of Who Hit John along with your two-dollar gold piece for the hour and we'll see if you have a chance to stay alive while seeking your justice."

"Thank you, sir. I'll be there."

I started to turn and leave, then my chin dropped as he snaked a little sheriff's model up and holding it by the barrel he brought it down hard on the back on the hand of the fella in city clothes.

His voice was low and ominous, and he glared at the fella. "You placed a bet. Keep your hands off it or you might lose one...hand, not the bet."

As the fella rubbed the reddened back of his hand with the other, he nodded. "Sorry," he mumbled. And Holliday went back to dealing.

Of course, I had spent many hours horseback and being a smithy knew the quirks and habits of horseflesh, but I'd seldom fired a rifle and never a shotgun while horseback. If the gray was to be a steady mount I figured I'd best get him accustomed to the crack of a rifle handled by his rider. But I had a mission first.

Sheriff Hollis Beaumont's office was only a block north on Montezuma but as my total belongings were in the saddlebags and scabbards on the gray, I rode him rather than leave my worldly possessions unguarded. Pleased, I found the sheriff to be at his desk.

Still, he kept us cooling our heels in an outer office, which gave me a chance to study the wanted flyers pinned to the wall and pay particular attention to those which said, "known to run with the Cade Tolliver gang."

He, too, I knew as I'd often shod his horse and also made latches and hinges for a home he'd recently built.

Glancing up, he sat his pen aside. "Conn, you're out of the hospital. Clear thinking now, I hope?"

"Pretty clear. The doc said you called and wanted a statement from me."

"He also said your recollections might be fuzzy."

"I remember many little things that keep drifting in and out as time goes by. What have you learned?"

He studies me for a moment before answering. "Well, young man, I've learned you are stocking up as if to go on the hunt yourself. Ain't your job—"

"But it's sure as hell my concern, Sheriff. Don't even try to dissuade me."

"I can't stop you, but I can give you some advice. I believe it was the Cade Tolliver gang that robbed the stage. Them fellas shoot straight and don't mind back-shooting. I won't go after them without two dozen backing me up. I've appealed to Colonel Aspenwall at Fort Whipple for help. You said you thought they be five. If you saw five there was likely another two down the trail and two up the trail to stop any interference. I believe there's at least ten of them trade coats. They run with some half-breed Apache murderers and Mexican Bob Comacho and his brother Pedro. Pedro has a scar from ear to chin and Bob a slash of white hair on the right side. But...you're one man and—"

"And one man can travel light and fast and not raise much dust. I don't plan to ride into their camp and start smokin' up the place. As my pa used to say, I was born in the night but not last night. I can live off the land and I'm young. I got lots of time."

"And I can't talk you out of this fool's mission?"

I'm quiet for a moment before I answer. "Every morning I awake thinking Sarah Ann's bloody head is in my lap and my hands are dripping with her life's blood. It would take all the soldiers at Whipple to hold me back. And then I'd find a way."

"You're gonna die trying."

"Then I'm gonna die. I'd rather die trying than live knowing her filthy cowardly killers were out there spending her dowry on whiskey and whores...and the proceeds of the sale of Fentons... while Sarah Ann is in a cold grave."

He shakes his head and sighs deeply before he responds. "Well, Godspeed, son. We'll bury you a'side her if'n there's room."

Chapter Four

The gray and I worked our way a mile out of town, far enough a little gunfire wouldn't bother townfolk. The little two-barrel belly gun was only .30 caliber so I decided it would be the least offensive to the gray. I set him into a slow walk and pulled one off at a pile of rocks to my left, which set him into a couple of frog leaps to the right, but I quieted him quickly with some soothing blather and a few pats on the withers and neck. As I suspected he was no Army pony and not accustomed to the snap and crack of a firearm nor black powder smoke.

The next shot was to my right and this time he only took one leap to the left. And was even more quickly settled. I may have been fooling myself but it seemed he was learning.

Slipping the 73 from its scabbard, I levered one in and fired again to the left. I was not quite ready for the half dozen stiff-legged leaps he took straight on down the trail. He damn nigh left me behind on my butt in the rocks and dust.

This time I was not quite so gentle with my complaint and had some unkind words to say about his linage, loud enough they may have heard me back at the Palace...but he and I both settled down and my complaints turned to understanding and pats on withers and neck. Before I replaced the 73 I let him have a smell of the muzzle while I tried to convince him neither Mister Winchester's tool nor my use of it meant him any harm. He seemed to reconcile himself with that explanation.

This time it was the double twelve-gauge, again to the left. I first let him smell the muzzle of that firearm as we moved along the trail at a comfortable stride.

The boom of the twelve would be a true test.

So, I pulled one off.

I think I was as surprised and unsettled as he was as he went straight up in the air, landed stiff-legged so hard I feared he'd loosened my molars, leaped left over a small cholla cactus, then as I was almost reseated, cleared it again back the way he'd come as it was now on his right. On the third stiff-legged hop I was dislodged and to my chagrin landed too close to the only other cholla in the neighborhood and filled my left thigh with prickley's.

I guess the gray and I hadn't been friends long enough as he didn't wait around for me to chastise him, rather he took off back to town and I hoped back to his former home at Alleandro's, where he was confident a quarter bucket of oats awaited and no one would ignite gunfire near his large, tender, ears.

To add insult to injury it had clouded up and an early monsoon had me soaked before I was twenty steps into my shank's mare journey. Least it would drive the snakes into the nearest hole.

It was ten minutes of hard strides, at times with rain so hard I could barely see the two-track I followed. The good of it was the gray was waiting at the barn door of Alleandro's Hostelry. The bad was the knothead had stepped on and broken both reins of the new bridle he wore.

Alleandro himself was exiting the office door as I approached. He was a little sheepish as he joined the gray and me. "No one said he was a bucker," he said.

"I was testing him for gunfire then he tested me to see if I could stay in the saddle. He won that first contest. We'll make peace on down the trail somewhere."

"I got a couple of hands full of rolled oats——"

"No, sir. We ain't gonna reward him for leaving me afoot. He'll get well fed before I stake him out...but now is too soon. Another set of reins, please. Four bits each, right?"

He nodded.

"I'd borrow some pliers if you got some. He put me in range of a very unfriendly cholla."

He couldn't help but smile which didn't improve my mood, but then redeemed himself. "You sold your bed with the forge, I'd guess."

"I did. Bed, bedding, lantern, wash bowl, and pitcher, all in the back room."

"You can sleep in the barn and stall him. Guess I owe you that much for selling you a bucker. Don't founder him on my oats."

"Obliged," I said. "And I'll buy you a beer at the Palace soon as I pluck the rest of them cholla thorns outta my thigh."

He tipped his hat and headed out to get a beer down before the free one.

I dropped my trousers and long johns in a stall and went to work on the thorns. Damn things seem as hungry as a starved snake and seem to keep burrowing in long after the first poke. I pulled them best I could but was sure they'd go to festering. Alleandro had a half bucket of fat of some kind to use on the horse's hooves, so I rubbed down the thigh with that and only then did I favor the gray with a couple of handfuls of oats.

I had a selfish motive wanting to go back to the Palace as it was the town meeting place with the truth likely far outrun by rumor, but a wise and doubting sage could likely winnow the chafe from the wheat.

Hollis Beaumont, the sheriff, had speculated the robbers and murderers were the Cade Tolliver gang, and if they operated around Yavapai County someone would know something about them and their whereabouts. I still had a pocket full of money and it was my intent to ply them that frequented the Palace with alcohol so the information would flow out of their pie holes after the whiskey flowed in.

Montezuma Street, coming to be known as Whiskey Row, separated the plaza with its courthouse nearly centered from the row of saloons and hurly gurdy pleasure palaces on the west side. The trees and shade of the plaza, and a few benches and stone tables, made it a meeting place for them who didn't partake of the sins offered on the west side. And for them who couldn't afford it. Dark comes late in Arizona and the Palace wouldn't yet be full of gamblers and whiskey drinkers so I wandered around the plaza then hobnobbed with them playing dominos, whist, and cribbage. I lost two bits to an old boy who looked as if he couldn't throw a horseshoe five feet much less to the stake forty feet from pit to pit. He double-ringed the last toss and I tipped my hat to him as I passed over the coin.

It was time to see if I could obtain some information so I could put to use what Doc Holliday was to teach me on the morrow.

I dodged a dray loaded with clattering-empty beer barrels and another with lumber while crossing Montezuma and shoved through the batwings...and as was usual the place was full of drovers, miners, drummers and townsmen. Two ladies whose pleasures could not be bought—although they had repeated offers—served the tables and two soiled doves worked the smoky room.

Alexis Towbridge was behind the bar as usual

and I tipped my hat to him as I headed for the back of the room where an upright piano was being beat to death by a fat man and another as skinny as the piano player was fat plucked a banjo. Even with the high ceilings smoke hung near down to eye level as half the men wrapped their lips around fat cigars and the other half chewed and spit, so every eight feet along the bar and next to tables was another brass spittoon. White towels hung under the front of the beautiful Brunswick bar on brass hooks and a brass foot rail ran the length of it. The center of the back bar featured a four-by-five-foot painting of a reclining lady with generous proportions, a representation of womanhood that assured that few local churchgoing women would grace the place with their presence even if in search of a wayward husband.

Four faro tables were full of players as was a wheel of chance, a table playing brag, one of three-card-monte, and one of five-card draw poker. So, eight tables plied their hard-earned from the crowd. Not to speak of the stairway in the rear that kept the two doves busy heading for upstairs cribs. Out the back of the alley stood side-by-side privies, but by the smell, men full of beer didn't always wait for room to do their business, although pissing in public was a crime in Prescott.

I found room at the bar and Alexis yelled from the other end, "Beer?" and I nodded. He came my way as I glanced to the side and realized I was elbow to elbow with Deputy Marshal Virgil Earp. Earp appeared to be near forty but had the manner of an even older fella, I guess he felt age fit the job of lawman. As soon as my beer landed and Alexis scooped up my dime, I toasted Deputy Earp and asked, "Mr. Earp, can I stand you to a whiskey?"

Chapter Five

"On the job, young fella," Earp said, "but thanks."

I'm sure I was less than ten years younger but accepted his comment and continued, "Can I bother you for some information?"

"Why not? Got to go on my rounds in a few minutes but I got a little time. What's your problem?"

"No problem, sir, just a question or two."

"Spit 'em up."

"What do you know about this Tolliver bunch that's been plaguing folks with robbing and killing?"

He studied me a moment, then asked,

"What's your interest? You a new reporter for *The Arizona Miner* or a dime novel writer?"

"No, sir. I was harmed by them, or so I've come to believe. I know you're a city marshal, but my wife was murdered out near Iron Springs—"

He gave me a silent nod. "We have reason to believe that was the Tolliver gang. We're on the watch for them if they show up in town."

"Where do those hooligans hole up?"

"Sheriff Beaumont is hot after them boys. They are the worst dregs of the territory and you should stand by and see what transpires."

"Would you?" I asked him, straight out.

He couldn't help but smile. Then got a more serious expression. "I don't believe your lady would want you skinned and scalped or worse, so you should see what transpires, or"—he gave me a nod—"or join a posse should it be called for."

"I'd have thought it would have been called for days ago."

He nodded, which I took for agreement, then leaned a little closer. "As most of their robbing has been on the road to Wickenburg I'd guess, should I be on the hunt for them, they be holed up in Skull Valley or nearby."

"Anything more specific?"

"I'd see the Johanson's out at the Skull Valley

Trading Post. If anyone knows more, it'd be Gustav and Anna Johanson. Them boys are supplying up somewhere and that would be the place if they are holed up out that way. Tell those good folks Virgil Earp said howdy."

"I will. Thank you, sir."

I got a nod, and he added, "I'll take that drink you run across me off duty."

"And you'll have it."

I'd gotten exactly what I wanted from Deputy Earp, then saw Alleandro at the wheel of chance, ordered another beer from Alexis, and headed his way. "Here's that beer I promised," I said, but he waved me off to wait as he watched the wheel.

"Damn the luck," he said, then turned to me and grabbed the beer. "Second time the wheel stopped one number short of mine."

"Anything need tending to at the barn? I'm headed out."

"Keep the riffraff outta my haystacks. Them bums all smoke and I don't want them burning down the place."

"I'll police for you," I said and waved as I headed for the batwings. I stepped behind Holliday's faro table and leaned down. "See you in the morning."

He waved me off as he was concentrating on the deal.

It was a good time for my leaving as I noticed Rafe Macintosh and his wild brother, the youngest of the Macintosh clan, Murdoch, eyeing me from across the room. Murdoch was as big as his older brother but much better looking, even as a redhead with a ruddy complexion always burned from the sun. I knew him to be only slightly younger than myself. He wore his revolver low and strapped down like he fancied himself a gunman and I was in no mood to find out his competency as I had a mighty grudge to settle. His attention was divided between me, his brother, and a dove he had an arm around. I'd met her strolling around the plaza and could understand his interest.

So, I beat a trail without meeting their murderous gaze.

I awoke early in my bed of hay with a rooster standing on the sill of the hayloft's loading window high above and announcing to the world that the sun is rising and it's time to get moving... so I did. After a visit to the privy I was at the trough between two paddocks at the rear of Alleandro's with my shirt and sox hanging on a fence post nearby and my long John's top hanging behind me while I took advantage of a bar of lye soap my host kept near at hand, when my host arrived.

"How'd you do at the Palace last night?" I asked after we'd traded nods.

"Should'a left with you. Lost two dollars a dime a spin. You missed the excitement?"

That stopped me from lathering up. "How so."

"That Macintosh...the youngest...traded insults with some cowhand and then beat him at the draw and shot him about liver high. He died on the way to the docs."

"Who was the cowhand?"

"Nobody seems to know. So far he's Mr. John Doe."

I was quiet for a moment then sighed and offered, "Too damn bad and sad for the cowhand. Did Earp arrest Macintosh?"

"He was off on his rounds, but Macintosh left word he'd come on into the city marshal's office this morning to give a statement, and others said they'd give depositions it was mutual combat... although Macintosh prodded him into drawing. Cowhand didn't clear the holster."

"I know Murdoch well, woulda slapped him silly myself many times had I not cherished his sister. He's a loudmouth but can handle a six-gun. Fact it, it's my belief he'll bring grief to the family. You had breakfast?" I asked.

"Beans and biscuits, I'm *muy bueno*."

"Okay I leave the gray here until after I eat?"

"Leave him all day if'n you're a mind to. If you stay the night again it's four bits which includes a rub down and dollop of oats."

"I'll be on my way before noon and thank you for your hospitality."

"Ma Hoyt's has the best sourdough hotcakes and side pork in the territory."

"Know it well," I say as I pull on my long johns and the still-damp socks and shirt.

Ma Hoyt's is a clapboard-fronted tent with the kitchen out back. The stove consists of a covered river stone six by three-foot brazier with a sheet of iron on one side and grate on the other. It was my work, the grate. Beyond a few paces is a privy and a four-foot high, four deep, fence of mesquite encloses the brazier, a thirty-foot square of fence fuel that could likely keep the brazier in fuel for a year.

Mama must have married a Hoyt as she's as Mexican as a tortilla and brown as a bean and hasn't missed a meal since she was only a wish in her mama's eye.

Side pork sizzles on one end of the grill, a dozen flapjacks brown on the other, a two-gallon pot of *frijoles* bubbles on the fire, and I'd guess they don't need a pile of mesquite coals to be hot as she's crumbling a hand full of dry red peppers in with stubby fingers about the size of corn cobs.

I pass through eight tables to the back to watch her and shake my head. Just the steam from the pot is making my eyes water. Ma Hoyt has forearms the size of my thighs and thighs the size of my waist. It amazes me how quickly and accurately she works. She can be flipping flap jacks with a spatula in one hand and breaking a cackle berry on the other end of the grill with the other, one-handed without a trace of shell. All while singing some Mexican ditty and entertaining the customers.

She glances up and seeing a new customer, yells over her shoulder, "Juanita, take *Señor* Donahey's order."

A pretty young girl who I know to be Ma Hoyt's daughter hurries out of the privy, pauses to wash her hands using a white pitcher and bowl on a little table backed up to the privy wall, then hurries on.

"You sit?" she asks.

"I sit. Short stack sourdough cakes, side pork, coffee."

"No *huevos*?"

"No, thank you, Juanita. Honey, if some's in the pot."

I take my time eating as I have hours to kill before meeting Holliday. I know that Ma Hoyt knows everything that happens in Prescott and probably a dozen miles around. When she closes on Sunday, after mass, I know she and Juanita work at Governor Fremont's home as laundress and though I know she acts as if she's deaf, she hears every comment. When things slow down, I wander out to the stone brazier.

She speaks while continuing to work, "So sorry for your trouble, Señor."

"Mama, I know you know the gossip on everyone in the territory. Have you heard any talk of this Tolliver bunch?"

She's quiet for a moment, I'm sure weighing if she wants to get involved. I haven't traded more than a few words with her in the years I'd been at Fenton's but it's always been cordial and I've been a steady customer.

Finally, she glances up. "I no mess in *gringo* business, Señor Donahey."

"And I wouldn't ask you to, but I know the

Macintosh family came here often and you wouldn't let Sarah Ann's killers—"

"And Miss Sarah was kind to us and once helped Juanita with her reading of English." Her tone hardened. "But you did not hear this from me, *comprendo?*"

"Not a word."

"The one they call Mexican Bob...a *mucho mucho mucho malo hombre*...he is sweet on the *muchacha*, Elena, who lives and works at the Skull Valley Trading Post. The Johanson family took her in seven or more years ago—Elena only eleven —when her mama and papa fell to the Mescalero. It is said Señor and Señora Johanson live in fear of Mexican Bob and his *amigos*. And you should as well."

"Thank you, Mama. I'm indebted."

"Go with God, young Donahey. I will light candles for you."

I left a dollar for the fifty-cent meal and headed to the plaza to see what, if any, gossip I could pick up.

It's amazing what you can learn over a game of checkers or dominos, or while pitching horseshoes.

Chapter Six

Tyrone Peabody wouldn't play dominos unless you bet a penny a point and lay at least two bits on the stone table before the draw, but he was a talker and like Mama Hoyt had big ears and knew all that went on in town, particularly in the houses of ill repute as he had the contract to keep four of them in firewood. And the ladies working there heard every brag known to man...the problem was winnowing the brag from the bull. Tyrone seemed as old as the mesquite he provided and his face, lined like an alligator juniper's bark, showed his years...but he could still wield an axe and crosscut with the best of them. I knew he'd been a prospector before a woodcutter and covered most of the Yavapai territory if not all of southern Arizona territory.

I pony'd up my quarter and took a seat across from him. He cackled and brayed like a donkey, then asked with a toothless grin, "You back for another shellacking?" and mixed the fancy ivories up. He only played with his own set and I couldn't help but wonder if they were marked in some way but could never challenge him.

Not wasting any time, I asked, "If a fella was going out Skull Valley way and wanted water and graze for his critters, where would he best camp?"

"That's fifteen," he said as he crossed my five with a double five and picked up the points. He marked them as he answered, "Dead mule canyon has a fine spring about a mile east up the draw from the road just when you get into the cedars, and another higher yet in the ponderosas. You can even find some bunch grass on up above...but, younger, that country's been picked at by the best, myself included."

"Not prospecting, just looking to camp out away from folks for a while."

"Heard you had some trouble...but that's not welcome country. It's no place to lay up and lick your wounds. I'd go south, up higher in on the mountain twixt here and black canyon."

We played and talked for a while until I figured I'd better head out to Quinton's Livery to get my lesson. I had to add thirty-two cents to my two bits to pay off my losses, but had gotten the location of four good water holes, so it was worth it.

As I got up to leave, he suggested, "Dead Mule branches 'bout a mile east of the road. If a fella took the south branch he'd see a rock shelf a few hundred yards up the trail. In that shelf is a big ol' cave. Good shade and a trickle of water where a few souls could hole up. But a smart pilgrim wouldn't just ride up on the camp…might get shot out of the saddle."

I gave him a nod. "Tyrone, you're a fine friend…even if you do take my money in dominos. I'm indebted." And I strode off.

I'd almost forgotten I was to bring a bottle of Who Hit John but knew one of the houses of ill repute off the alley along the way would sell a bottle and swung into Polkinghorn's Pleasure Palace. Two girls sat in the upstairs window, and both gave me the come on as I climbed the stairs but I ignored them and walked straight to the little four seat bar. "A bottle of Who Hit—"

"Don't carry it," said the smiling chubby lady

who hurried to serve me. "You got a favorite?" she asked.

"Who Hit—"

"Not whiskey, junior. Favorite of one of my ladies."

"Sell me a bottle and I'll decide."

"Got Rattlesnake or Preacher's Promise."

"Price?" I asked.

"Two dollars a quart for the snake and three for Preachers."

I forked two dollars out of my pocket and she handed the bottle over. "Thanks," I said over my shoulder as she yelled after me.

"You said you'd pick a lady."

I waved over my shoulder and lied like a lawyer. "I may be back after I drink up some courage."

Quintons was on the north side of town near Granite Creek. I probably should have returned to Alleandro's and saddled the gray as I'd promised to be out of there by noon, but I felt I needed the walk and it was a fine day.

Even at that I was a few minutes early and to my surprise Holliday was already there playing a hand of cribbage with Cory Quinton, who owned the place.

"You come with a good eye and steady hand?" he asked.

"And a full box of fifty," I answered.

"I done set a row of peach cans on a log down by the creek. Let's go."

We didn't get far when he sat on a stump and motioned to me to plop down on a nearby rock.

"I was wanting to learn to outdraw the other fellow," I said.

He shook his head as if disgusted. "First thing you should know is it ain't the fella who clears leather first, it's the fella who puts an ounce of lead in the other fella's brisket."

He rose and faced me, pulled his coat tail back behind his holster on the left side, and I didn't think he was going to draw as he patted his right shoulder with his left hand, then to my surprise he dropped the hand to an unseen single action Peacemaker on his right side, and had it on me in a flash. It was a move to confuse the other fella and it sure as the devil is mean did.

He laughed, then coughed up a wad and spat, then eyed me. "Conn, there ain't no such thing as a fair street or saloon fight. If another fella means to kill you, dead set to make you dead, then you need to use every advantage. You might note I always have two revolvers on my person and always where I can draw one with my butt flat on the chair, which means a cross draw...as I make my living with my butt flat on the chair." I'm nodding as I listen, so he continues. "If I know trouble is on the way, it's the scattergun the weapon of choice for many fellas. You got one?"

"Yes, sir, back with my gear."

"You got a belly gun?"

"Yes, sir, one that fits fine in my boot."

"Fine in your boot but worthless in a gun battle. You think the other fella is gonna wait for you to hoist your pant leg?"

"No, sir. Guess not."

"Then you keep it in your coat pocket opposite your holstered revolver."

"Okay, why?"

"Because you're gonna have a hand in that pocket and your normal draw hand on your lapel or in the other pocket like you got no idea about drawing."

"How's that gonna help?"

"'Cause you're gonna plug the other chap with the belly gun while he's thinking he has the advantage as he's thinking you'll have to get your drawing hand out of your pocket or off your lapel and your coat tail back before you can get a hand on that revolver. Odds are he left honor behind with his mother's milky tit."

"So, I draw the belly gun I've already got a hand on?"

"No," he says, to my surprise.

"You shoot that dumb galoot with your hand still in your pocket on that belly gun. Yes, you're gonna put a hole in your coat but that's lots better than a hole in your brisket and your blood pumpin' all over some sawdust-covered barroom floor until your heart stops. Now, let's see if you can hit something besides your own flat foot. Just in case you run low of shots in the belly gun."

He only had me shoot two spinners full of shells then complimented me. "You're a fine shot from twenty-five feet."

"Thank you," I said, but he interrupted me before I could continue.

He coughed again then he added, "But a peach can is not a man with a .44 looking to blow you out into the street then come out and spit chaw in your face while you're on your back in the road apples. If a fella reaches against you, don't wait. You can argue the right or wrong of it with the judge but only if you live to argue."

"Yes, sir. I owe you two dollars."

"And a bottle, and a drink at the Palace should you have time. By the time we get there, I'll just have time for some cold cuts before I take my table and give the pilgrims a shot at taking the houses money. You got that bottle of Who Hit John?"

"Didn't have the Who, but I brought a bottle of Rattlesnake, how-some-ever I left it on the table back there with Mr. Quinton."

"Humph," Holliday managed. "Som'bitch likely drank it."

I couldn't help but ask, "How old are you, Doc?"

"Twenty-eight." Then he smiled. "But I been rode hard and put away wet more often than most fellows been to the privy...besides this damned consumption ages a fella."

"You got near ten years on me. I truly appreciate you taking the time."

"My pleasure, Conn. You seem like a nice young fella. That said, your task means you set nice aside. Nice and believing the other fella has an ounce of nice in him will assure you won't see another birthday. You'll have time for nice when your task is complete."

We left, him on horseback and me shanks

mare, but feeling like I'd been at the master's feet and might have a slightly better chance to avenge my Sarah...and I damn sure meant to do so.

Tomorrow the gray and I are headed for Skull Valley.

Chapter Seven

I went ahead and paid Alleandro the four bits for stalling and graining the gray so long as he let me sleep in the hay again. But I was going to have to start watching my purse as I was now unemployed and money was getting scarce. I planned to remedy that as I was sure Cade Tolliver and crew would have a satchel full of my money, Sarah's dowry, and probably the pokes of dozens of others they'd robbed and murdered.

That said, if Sheriff Beaumont is right, I'm sure there are at least nine no-goods standing, armed and angry, between me and that bounty, and if I wade my way through them I only plan on keeping what I lost. The rest I'll return to the law to repay them that lost it, if any of them are alive or have heirs. Of course, the odds of me wading my way through nine *pistoleros*, if nine is the number, is damn slim and slim has likely left town before I even set out.

Alleandro bade me goodbye and good luck and looked at me with a shake of his head like I was already on my back in a pine box on display at the diggers—I half expected him to do the sign of the cross—but my anger overcame any fear and I set out with a handful of jerky and canteen of fresh water from my host's pump. The day, warm and pleasant. The two-track road, slightly north of west out of Prescott, lined with pines and junipers. The road was quiet and nearly clear, passing and tipping my hat to only a couple of drovers heading to town and one farm wagon with sacks of grain and potatoes. I bought a few to top off my saddlebags investing only a dime. The two pounds of grain were loaded by the farmer into a fine cloth sack and the potatoes loose. I commented on the sack and the farmer said his wife sewed them from larger grain sacks and he sold them, full of grain, to a grocer who sold them for chicken feed.

Chewing on a raw spud, I passed the spot where the Concord had been held up and my new wife murdered and noted the remnants of the six-inch thick pine tree still lay on either side of the road. Then it dawned on me, why had the road agents come so far from Skull Valley to do their dirty deed when the road in a few miles turned south and ran for miles much closer to where I suspected they holed up. And did they stop at Chauncey and Martha McNab's Iron Springs Trading Post? After another quarter mile, I tied the gray at the post's hitching rail and made my way inside. It was a sturdy building of eight-inch ponderosa logs, split shingles—probably cedar—with a handsome six-foot wide river stone fireplace and a couple of windows of real glass, six panes each. The door at the back, I suspect, led to living quarters.

Two near twenty-foot-long free-standing shelves, three deep, were spotted with canned goods and supported small bins full of potatoes, carrots, turnips, and dried apples. Tin goods, plates and cups and some cooking gear near filled one shelf. A deep pile of woven wool blankets and rugs snuggled in a corner, likely traded from the distant Navajo or Hopi tribes. One end of one bank of shelves featured ammunition of various calibers and cans of black powder, fuses, and tins of Hercules blasting caps. Another showed off bolts of cloth, thread, yarn, needles, tatting and crocheting goods. The walls were covered with hanging items, hats, some heavy coats left over from winter, and traps of various sizes from rat to bear. A few pelts hung, taking up one wall. Coyote, wolf, bear, deer, elk, and smaller skunk, marten and even some weasel, seemed well tanned and ready for use.

Chauncey McNab strode out from behind the counter and extended a bony hand, which I took with some caution worried I might crush his, his balding head only shoulder high to me. But he had a cocky walk and manner befitting a game rooster. He seemed to size me up as he gazed over spectacles. Martha McNab poked her head out of the back where the odor of biscuits wafted.

Chauncey wasted no time seeing what he could pry out of my pocket. "You looking to stock up?"

"Just came from Prescott—"

"My prices match theirs."

"No doubt. I do see some items I might favor, should we come to a meeting of the minds."

"Missus is just pulling a pan of biscuits out of the oven. You better try a couple lathered in gravy before they float off her plate and out the window. Two bits."

I'd planned to bean up at the stage stations,

two more of which lay between Prescott and Wickenburg, and her biscuits were making my chops water. Since I was going to pry him for information and likely wouldn't have another chance at home cooked until I reached the Skull Valley Trading Post, I gave him a nod. "Coffee included?"

He gave me an impish smile and a merchant's answer. "All you can drink for another nickel."

"You'll join me?"

"I got chores but I never miss her biscuits, warm from the oven. We'll throw in another with some honey...particularly if you're gonna stock up."

A small table nestled up against one of the windows. It hosted three chairs and after pouring coffee, Martha reappeared with three plates heaped with biscuits and gravy. I had some concern for the chair she took as although she was no taller than Chauncey she barely fit through the kitchen door...this wasn't her first heaping plate of biscuits and gravy.

Wasting no time as soon as she settled into the groaning chair, I asked, "Y'all had some trouble just up the road a few days ago."

Chauncey answered, "We try and keep our

noses out of what happens beyond that door," and he motioned to the entrance.

"Hard to do if some hooligans stick their heads in your door. Since those bandits seem to work the road outside, I imagine they're customers."

Martha kept her eyes down on her plate and Chauncey merely gazed at me, both responses I found telling.

So, I continued in an assertive knowing manner. "Smart fellas like the Cade Tolliver bunch wouldn't berate or steal from a good source of supplies, like your post here. I'm sure they know you'd book no trouble. They come in often?"

I'd already judged Chauncey being a bit of a blowhard—I'd come to know small fellas often make up for size with braggadocio—and he couldn't help but take the bait. He puffed up like a rooster about to crow before he spoke. "We ain't judge and jury and I sell to anyone, including Indians, should they come in hat in hand. I done shot dead a couple of drovers who tried to steal from us...caught 'em in the chicken coup. So, the word got out...you don't mess with the McNabs should you wanna keep body and soul together."

"I judged that right off. You'd be no one to mess with." I gave him my best smile.

"Thank the Lord," Martha said, without looking up from her already half-empty plate.

Chewing a couple of bites before I continued, I asked, "So, when was the last time Tolliver and his bunch came in...hat in hand of course."

"They was here right before that passenger wagon was robbed. Bought a couple of boxes of .44-40 and ate a whole apple pie and paid good money and even tipped Martha a dime. Like I say, we ain't judge and jury."

"Wouldn't expect you to be."

"Tolliver plays the gentleman but the Mexican he runs with and the half-breed—"

"Half-breed?"

"Goes by Carlos...and I heard Tolliver call him Apaza, but he's half Apache, Yavapai, Pima...or who knows. Ugly lout with a pearl eye somebody poked out. He pocketed a piece of hard candy that day and I traded sharp words with Tolliver and he paid the penny. Like I said I don't abide no thievin'."

I gave him a nod as I lathered my extra biscuit in honey, then asked, "How many were they and did you know the names of the others?"

He dropped his head and eyed me over his

spectacles. "You the law? I already went through all this with Sheriff Beau...what's his name... Beaumont."

"Not the law, just passing the time. I'm headed to Wickenberg and it'd be good to know who to fight shy of."

"Humph," he said, but continued. "They were a bunch but only four came inside. Tolliver knows I get hot under the collar they be more than we can watch."

"No guess as to how many?"

"Eight or so, maybe nine. Filled the hitching rail outside. I was busy watching them what came inside."

I nodded, figuring I was pushing my luck as he was getting suspicious of my motives. "How about we talk powder and blasting caps...and maybe one of those bear traps over there hanging on the wall?"

I left with what might serve as another weapon or two to add to my armory. I would have to buy me a mule or pack horse if I added more goods.

It would be twenty miles before I entered the Skull Valley and another few to that trading post.

I damn sure had to be watchful from now on.

Chapter Eight

I'd made this trip once before when old man Fenton had me accompany him to Wickenberg and just south of there to Vulture Mine that wanted several dozen fittings pounded out, used to tie square posts, cribbing blocks, headers, and caps together. It wasn't old man Fenton needed my help or advice, he was worried about his health as he'd had two attacks and wanted a friendly face near if'n he had another. It wasn't like I knew every bump in the road but I have a general feel for it. After traveling through the country, I got curious about how it got the name Skull Valley and found it came by it honestly. Before the white man the Pima and the Yavapai had a huge battle there and the Yavapai bodies were left to rot. It's said even now a plow turning land will occasionally turn up a skull.

Maybe it's appropriate as a place of death as I plan to add to the toll.

May's a fine time in Arizona with an ample supply of green grass in the blooming desert, lots of wildflowers, the land fresh, blooming and colorful. Most new settlers are surprised when summer heat comes to the land late in June, and even later in July or August the dry desert is swept with rainstorms called monsoons and it's known to rain inches in a few hours. The unwary are caught in flood swept ravines or they set out thinking plenty of water will be available but the desert swallows it up almost as soon as it hits the ground.

And it can be an unforgiving place, not only the heat but every damn thing seems to want to bite you, sting you, poison you, burn you, poke you or eat you. Even in the heat it pays to wear canvas pants, sturdy boots, long sleeves, and a hat with a floppy brim wide enough to shade your shoulders. And you must care for your horse as being put afoot can kill you in a day when the heat comes in earnest and you can fry an egg on a granite rock.

I was fortunate to have a Yavapai friend, much

to the chagrin of his family and mine. I taught him to read and to pound iron and he taught me a smidgen of the ways of the desert, things most white men never learn even after a lifetime in the territory. His name was Yahoochi, best I could spell it, but I merely called him Hooch. Unfortunately, we seldom ventured out of the cedar, or juniper, country but for two or three times when hunting deer we'd ridden far enough west to have to dodge the cholla, organ pipe, barrel, prickly pear cactus and enjoy the shade of saguaro forty feet or more tall. Still, I knew I could live in the Sonoran a lifetime and still not know half what the Yavapai did. They'd lived there so long God forgot where he put them.

My friend was killed by a neighbor rancher who saw him riding through his cattle and figured he was stealing—likely he was coming to see me. The rancher was found guilty. His punishment? He had to pay Hooch's family five head of cattle. He picked out cows past their prime. I knew Hooch to be an honest young man and his family to be fine people. He would never accept anything from me without returning something he considered of equal value. I was not surprised when the rancher, much later, went missing and was never found, and to be truthful I never liked the Dutchman and did not bemoan his fate. As ye sew so shall ye reap. I'm sure it was them who got him, but even then they didn't get something of equal value to my way of thinking.

Five or six miles from Iron Springs I passed Jack's, which was a Prescott-Wickenburg-Maricopa Wells Express Company station and likely fifteen more miles to the next, Skull Valley Trading Post, but pushed on.

I'll give the gray this, he's a fine walker. Skull Valley is sandwiched between the pines and high country and the cactus and lower desert. A south-flowing river wanders through it, lined with cottonwoods. My road has now turned south, and I'll soon enter the valley and with luck can water the gray in the river.

The weather was mild which made the hunting much easier. A small herd, or sounder, of Javelina crossed the road in front of me, spooking the gray a little, the papa boar probably near fifty pounds, a half dozen shoats only three or four. But Javelina is not on the top of my culinary list, in fact I plumb dislike the critter. I'd prefer rattlesnake to a javelina chop. I jumped two buck deer and thought about pulling the 73 from its scabbard as they only ran fifty yards before settling down to graze again, but I figured staying quiet the wise tack to take. I was looking to attract a bevy of bad guys but had no interest in being drygulched by them as I plodded along.

I was only a hundred paces shy of what I remembered to be a river crossing when I heard the hoofbeats and rattle of a wheeled vehicle coming up behind me. I reined off and behind a clump of buckbrush until I saw it was the Prescott-Wickenberg Concord coming at an easy canter. I reined back beside the road and the whip pulled rein and they stopped twenty feet short and the shotgun guard yelled out.

"Your intent?"

I found that a bit strange but with what had recently happened when I was a passenger, didn't laugh.

"Just traveling, friend. No evil intent from this pilgrim."

"That you, Conn?" the whip yelled out.

"Yes, sir. Conn Donahey. Who's asking?"

"Terrill McNaulty, just mustered out from Fort Whipple. You might recall the colonel sent me to Fenton's a year or so ago to buy a couple of dozen mule shoes and you helped me out. Now I got me Toby Willard's job, God rest his soul." He pulled his hat off as he spoke, re-centered it then added, "This be Chance Tucker, got him Oscar's job."

"Howdy." I tipped my hat to him.

Chance doffed his wide-brimmed felt, reseated it, and asked, "I don't guess you've seen any sign we'd like to know about."

"Passed a couple of farmers and a couple of cowhands other side of Iron Springs. That's about it."

"Well, keep a sharp eye. You've had enough trouble. Come to think on it, you can tie that gray on the back and ride with us you got a mind to?"

"Kind of you, Terrill, but the quiet lonely suits me."

"We won't be stopping at the Skull Valley Trading Post 'cept to switch teams, running a mite late, or I'd buy you three fingers."

I laughed. "Staying dry unless I've a need to be social. Thanks, I'll take a rain check."

"Stay safe," he said and cracked his whip over the four-up like he'd been driving team since old enough to spit. Likely he was a teamster with the Army. They kicked up dust going by and splashed through the twenty-foot wide, six-inch deep river, made a bend beyond and were soon out of sight.

I crossed the river twice more, watering the gray, before I saw the Skull Valley Trading Post in the distance, A log building with another fifty-foot distance behind, probably living quarters, and a privy in between. As I got closer I spotted a small barn and corral deeper in the junipers. A tendril of smoke snaked its way skyward from the post's rock chimney, and another from the house. Chickens pecked in the yard between and two goats surrounded by four kids roamed freely eating anything green in their path.

I'd been riding with my Colt in its saddle holster, but seeing two saddle horses at the rail near the door, slipped it out and into my belt holster as I dismounted. I tied the gray as far from a palomino and red roan as I could and noted neither animal carried a bedroll and their saddlebags looked empty. Neither animal was lathered nor breathing hard, so they'd not been ridden hard nor long, or they'd been rail-tied for a good long time. Nor was there a pack animal in sight. Their riders were locals, not travelers. Both saddles had rifle boots but both were empty. Whoever was inside carried their long guns with them or left them home.

So, taking Doc Holliday's advice, after nestling the Colt in my belt holster, I slipped the coach-gun from its scabbard, checked the loads, and only then headed inside. The place was stocked with the normal for a distant country store: canned and sacked goods, guns and ammo, feed and leather goods, lanterns and coal oil, and a rack of ready mades. The counter sported a cash box, chaw cutter, wide-mouthed mug full of hard candy, a jar of pickled eggs, and one of hard sausages. The eggs were priced at two cents and the sausages at four. A small basket of fresh eggs rested near, priced at a penny each. The counter continued fifteen feet to the back wall, only it rose to become an eight-man saloon bar with stools, three spittoons, and four white towels hanging below the polished pine.

It was as pretty as the two standing there drinking four-finger glasses of whiskey were ugly. The prettiness of the polished bar was only exceeded by the beauty of the raven-black-haired beauty serving the two. As I entered, she yelled to the rear, "Mama Anna, a customer." Then flashed a smile at me. "Welcome, sir."

"Thank you," I replied as the two at the bar eyed me carefully.

The girl was either half-breed Mexican or some very light stock. Her hair at first appeared raven-wing black but as the sun from a window reflected off it I caught strands of red. The two at the bar were dressed Mexican with calzoneva trousers, silver conchos down the outside seam. Wide belts each featured a revolver in a holster on one side—tied down like a fella who thought himself a shooter would have it—and a sheath and foot long-bladed knife on the other. Sombreros hung from their chin straps on a rack near the front door, with serapes on wall hooks nearby. As I suspected, lever action rifles leaned on the bar in easy reach.

Both of them rested hands on the butts of the revolvers on their hips as I strode to the far end of the bar, as far as I could get from them. As I leaned on the bar I propped the coach gun beneath the bar in easy reach.

I was pretty damn sure I was going to need it.

Chapter Nine

After a glance, I ignored them as the lass came from them to across from me. I could understand Mexican Bob's infatuation with her as she was dark, beautiful, and enticing to use a polite word.

Her smile would stagger a weak man, her voice a little low and husky. "I guess mama is out back. Papa is watering the last team to stop. Your pleasure, sir?"

As the Mexicans were still eyeing me, I'd guess with suspicion, I ordered to make them believe I was a *paisano*, "Pulque or aguardiente, whichever."

"Two bits for either, I have both, finely made, but I have Irish Whiskey all the way from the emerald isles...four bits for three fingers?"

"Pulque," I said, dropping a silver quarter on the bar. She nodded and moved to the end near the Mexicans and snaked a clay jug with painted images of spiny green century plants adorning its sides, from under the bar.

"So"—from eight feet away, the Mexican nearest me nodded to me—"the young gringo likes the agave juice?"

It was the first time I saw him full face on, and was not surprised to see a puckered scar from ear to chin, like he'd drawn the short end of a knife fight. So, this is more than likely the gang member called Pedro, brother to Mexican Bob. I could feel the heat crawl up my backbone and the palm of my gun hand itched craving being filled with the bone grips of my Colt.

I merely nodded and reached for the small glass of pulque the girl sat before me. As I took a sip, he asked, "I have seen you before?"

And he likely has, unconscious on the ground next to my murdered wife. As I wore a neckerchief, he could not see the healing scab on the back of my neck. I glanced back at him, and lied as I asked, "Have you been to Chicago?"

"No, no, I have never been far away from Mexico. I have seen you here, in Apache country?"

I shook my head without really looking at him nor answering aloud.

So, he continued, "Are you a lawman, gringo?"

With that I laughed, and he furrowed his brow, now a little confused.

I shrugged. "We may have met in the Wickenberg *jusgado, amigo*. But I was not there as a lawman." I laughed again. "Maybe Yuma prison?"

"They could not jail me, *gringo*. Not enough *gringos* in Arizona territory to jail Pedro Comacho."

"If you say so, Pedro." I downed the pulque in a gulp and picked up the coach gun as if I was going to leave. But as I came even with him, I jammed the double barrel in his gut, cocking them both at the same time. The other, who I presumed to be Mexican Bob, still leaned with his belly against the bar.

But he spun and reached for his revolver a moment too late as I only had one hand on the shotgun and had drawn the Colt with the other, cocking it with the motion. His revolver was half pulled when I growled, "Pull and die, Bob." The white streak of hair on his right side was now plain to me, and it was all I could do not to split his gizzard with a .44-40 or worse, nine shotgun pellets.

He hesitated then let the revolver slip back in his holster. A fly lit on his nose and I could see he was smart enough not to try to wave it away with a hand.

Pedro, his voice cracking a little, managed, "Be very light on those triggers, gringo."

The girl stood behind them in my line of fire and the last thing I wanted was an innocent life on my hands—particularly one as beautiful as she. I planned on having plenty of guilty ones to plant. However, I didn't want the two of them to know I'd hesitate for any reason, so I snapped at her, "Go get your ma or pa."

She didn't pause but hurried for the back door and disappeared outside.

She was out of the line of fire, but as much as I wanted to see these two die, I couldn't bring myself to pull the trigger on two men with their hands half in the air. The thought came to me to have Johanson bind them and to haul them back to the law in Prescott. Maybe watching them hang would satisfy my lust.

So, I instructed, "Turn very slowly and place both hands as far as you can reach across the bar. I have no problem cutting you in half with this scatter gun, so please, please give me an excuse." I backed away so they couldn't slap the muzzle away should they be foolish enough to try and commanded, "Turn, now, slowly, and reach." And they did.

"Now, with your left hands, unhitch the gun belts and let them drop to the floor."

As they were doing so the girl entered, her father—adopted father, I guess—was close behind.

"What the hell is going on here?" the older man demanded.

I replied without taking my eyes off the Mexicans. "You're Mr. Johanson?"

"I am, and I own this place and I have a pistol trained on you so you'd better talk fast. You a lawman?"

Quickly glancing over I saw he had a revolver aimed at my midriff, so I answered quickly, "No, sir. I'm the fellow who was married to a beautiful young lady and these two were with a bunch of lowlifes who killed her and four others, and will damn sure wish they'd finished me off when they had the chance."

"Your name?" he asked.

"Conn...Conn Donahey, from Prescott."

I glanced again and saw that Johanson's wife had slipped in behind him.

"You should know, Conn Donahey," he began,

his voice steady, "the missus and I don't condone killing for any reason. We are of the Quaker persuasion. So, you're gonna let these fellas slip out the front door and ride with the wind."

"The hell—" I started, but he interfered.

"And there's no cussing in my establishment. You can catch up with these two some other time and place. No blood will be spilled in our place of business."

"You bind 'em up and I'll haul them to the law in Prescott."

"Which would likely result in their hanging. I've seen town juries find fellows guilty just 'cause they didn't like the cut of their jib. And hanging's as bad as bleeding out, so I'll pass on that option as well."

"No blood? Then I presume you don't mean to use that pistol you have pointed at me?"

"That is some different young man. If you intend to spill blood, then I must act to prevent it. Besides, there's some to be said for me shooting only one to prevent two from being shot."

I snorted. "That's by-God backward logic if I ever heard it."

"No matter. These two are going to walk on out—"

"Not with their firearms or pig stickers. If they reach, they'll die trying, and you, Mr. Johanson, will likely make a widow woman out of the missus. I'll stand down and so will you, and these two will walk out, but without their firearms and knives. Those are staying with me."

He didn't speak, but Mexican Bob did. He stood from leaning across the bar and headed for the door. "We will meet again, *gringo*. Only next time it will be you leaning across the bar or bleeding on the bar floor, and I will have your weapons."

Pedro followed suit, and they disappeared out the door. I holstered my revolver, and Johanson lowered his. We glared at each other while we listened to the pounding of horse hooves.

My mouth was so dry it was hard to speak, but I got it out, "You made a big mistake here, Mr. Johanson."

For the first time, Mrs. Johanson spoke up. "The young man is probably right, Gustav. That bunch doesn't know logic or fairness or kindness from cow patties and they'll be back with the others and you and me and maybe especially Elena will suffer...mark my words."

"You foolish woman, don't you see God's work was done here today? No blood was spilled."

Chapter Ten

I ignored Mr. Johanson and turned to his missus, "Where do they hole up?" I asked.

But before she could answer, Johanson cleared his throat and his voice rose an octave. "If I knew, I would not say. That would only lead to spilled blood."

I gave him a look that likely loosened his coffee-stained teeth before I spoke. "Mr. Johanson, those fellows killed my wife and four others. That's spilled blood, good, honest, God-fearing blood, not the blood of snakes and skunks. It's my belief there are nine of them to pay, so you go on and believe no blood should be spilled and I'll go on and figure it's two or maybe ten drops of theirs for every drop they've shed. I'm a smithy and I've done beat my plow shears into swords, as the good Lord instructed. You read what you want to read out of the Good Book and I'll read what I want to read and believe." He seemed a little taken aback, and in fact backed up a step or two as I continued.

"Saint Pete will judge us at the gates and we'll see who's right. Until then." I gave him my back and turned to Elena who'd walked behind the bar. "I'd like to buy a half dozen eggs."

"Humph," old man Johanson said, and spun on his heel and left.

"Happy to help you, Mr. Donahey," Elena said, and fished my dinner out of a basket on the bar. I filled my hat with eggs, but then she handed me a little muslin sack with a pull string I could hang on a saddle horn and I used it.

The girl, Elena, reached over and lay a hand on my forearm, centering eyes as black as midnight at the bottom of a coal mine, on mine. "*Via con Dio's*. Be very careful."

I merely nodded and she followed Mister Johanson out the back as Mrs. Johanson took her place behind the counter. As soon as the door shut the older woman leaned across the bar and in a near whisper, advised, "They always ride out as if going west into the desert, but I've seen them on the ridge, they circle back and hole up, as you say, somewhere west of us in the pines. Be careful. There's an ex-slave in their midst. He cooks and does Tolliver's bidding, came west with Tolliver from Alabama. He goes by Hector. He's a fine older man who's only there as he's forced to be. Like many of his ilk, he's forced by a former master to stay on. I pray they never return here. I fear for Elena."

She handed me a box of .44-40's and asked, "Will this help? A gift, Mr. Donahey."

I gave her one of my old pa's favorites, "May you be in heaven an hour before the devil knows you're dead. God bless you, ma'am."

She added as I headed for the door. "If you're gonna stop at Tyler Tate's, the next station, don't worry about running into that Tolliver gang. Tyler is a tough old bird, former lawman from Ellsworth and Dodge, Kansas. He won't tolerate those boys coming anywhere near his place and he don't have enough for them to care."

I nodded and waved again. But Tate's would have to wait. I planned to check out Dead Mule Canyon.

It was near dark and my gut was growling. I checked the track, and they had ridden out west but over hard ground and my intuition and old Tyrone the former prospector domino player had given me a lead on a cave to the west. A cave with fresh water and room for a dozen owlhoots to hide in comfort. The mouth of Mule Canyon, if what was told me was correct, was only a mile south of Skull Valley Trading Post where I now mounted up. The sun was touching the hills to the west and it'd be dark soon, so I gigged the gray into a lope and found a good game trail west along the north rim of the canyon. I was still in the junipers when I came across a flat with decent grass. It would be a dry camp but the gray had watered well in the river. I gathered some trash wood, enough for a small fire and dry enough not to smoke and announce my camp and whipped up the eggs in my tin bowl and had me an omelet and a couple of strips of jerky for supper while the hobbled gray grazed. The tin bowl, a tin cup, a small knife and fork, and a single man's eight-inch cast iron Dutch oven comprised my kitchen. When finished I scrubbed them with a handful of sand and wiped them clean with my handkerchief.

For the first time since Sarah Ann was murdered I had a full night's sleep, only awakening once when the gray whinnied at some critter in the brush. I guess being on the hunt for her killers soothed me somewhat. Of course, now they knew I was on the prod, thanks to old man Johanson turning Mexican Bob and Pedro out to run for their cohorts and give them the word.

I awoke with a dry mouth and a determined set to my jaw. Before the sun was peeking over the high mountains to the east I'd shaken out my boots to make sure the scorpions hadn't found a wet warm place to hole up and rolled up my canvas and packed and cinched up the gray.

Tyrone, the domino maestro, said the canyon branched, with the cave somewhere on the north facing south side of the south branch so I crossed over and found another game trail leading up to the ridge on that side.

Riding the ridge was a fool's errand as I'd be backlighted by what was a clear blue sky and I'd yet to come upon the rock ridge Tyrone had mentioned, so I dropped down to the brow of the hill and picked my way through the junipers until the hillside was spotted with pines.

It wasn't more than a mile before the rocky slope became too steep to traverse and soil turned to granite. The hard-shouldered rock ridge continued in layered granite on up into thick ponderosa pine forest and I figured that somewhere below me was the cave.

Although I could not see a tendril of smoke

my nose twitched with what I was sure was a tinge of savory frying bacon.

As Arizona territory has a way of doing, I could see clouds forming off to the south. Good chance by afternoon we'd be doused even with the sky now clear blue overhead. I'd worked the gray hard picking my way through the trees and rocks, making our own trail a good part of the time, and wanted to water him again and fill my canteen, so I hunkered down and staked him where he could find some shade from a pine and graze. I was praying for rain for two reasons. The gray and I could water, God grant us some puddles or runoff, and I could move off to the north, pick my way to an edge and find a view of the canyon bottom and with luck the mouth of the cave...and rain would drive anyone there inside and any lookouts to be less observant.

Figuring I might have to do a little snooping in the middle of the night I decided to take a snooze and spread my bedroll under a thick juniper and was about to doze off when the gray whinnied loud and long as if there was a mare on the wind.

His attention was to the north—the direction I figured the trouble lay—and his ears swiveled back and forth in that direction. So, I sat up with my back against the trunk, the coach gun in my lap, and waited. It wasn't a moment before a sow javelina and six shoats trotted by. So, I returned to my snooze.

Rain dripping on my nose awakened me.

The shadow of the pine the gray was staked near reached long and dark to the east. On rising, I noted the sun had touched the skyline to the west. The rain was hardly more than a drizzle but at least the wet ground would make for quiet creeping, so I sat out, this time with the 73, as any necessary shots would likely be from the ridge to the canyon bottom. But it wasn't my intent to stir up a hornet's nest. One or two hornets I'd be happy to take on, but not near a dozen.

It was a good hundred yards before the downhill became exposed granite and the hillside a cliff. Slowly I worked my way until I got as far as possible without a hundred-foot fall and studied the bottom of the canyon. I was not surprised to see a trickle of water winding its way northeast and coming from somewhere in the wall I couldn't make out, maybe seventy-five yards on upstream. No site of my targets from my perch but they were damn sure near as I could see a remuda of horses, twelve strong along with four mules. Only then I did make out a figure about twenty feet up the cliffside. He'd made himself a shelter from a slicker and was positioned so he could see far down the canyon. A lookout. From my position on the clifftop he was about a hundred-yard shot, an easy one for the 73 and me, but not knowing the lay of the land and the number and location of the enemy, it would be a fool's errand to drop him.

So, I bided my time and fervor.

And it was getting dark.

I started to make my way back, then stopped short. Damned if the sound wafting out of the canyon wasn't a fiddle playing some jaunty tune.

Enjoy it you gobs of chaw, I thought as I made my way back to my dry camp. Could be your last dance.

Chapter Eleven

Morning crept over my dry camp with the smell of dove weed and with the namesake critters, whitewings, winging overhead to make their way to the trickle in the canyon. Hooch had put me onto following doves and bees as a sure way to find water and the knowledge had served me many times since.

We hadn't had enough rain for puddles, so I was gonna have to make my way to the bottom of the canyon and the trickle or back down the ridge to the river and water the gray, but I figured I'd first see if there was movement in the camp. Now that I had a fair idea where the cave was, I knew it was either ride on in like I was a Roman Legion or cross to the other side of the canyon so I could eyeball the actual entrance.

After munching a handful of dried apples and a piece of hardtack and chasing it with half my canteen of water, and rolling up and tying my bedroll on my saddle, I didn't saddle up rather I found another spot and staked the gray out where he could graze another patch of green. Then I headed for the edge again to see what I could see from my high perch. I found the same spot as last night and parked myself, and the hooligans were again frying bacon the whiff of which made my mouth water. I couldn't see them but sure as Hell's hot could smell them.

I hadn't been in the crevice watching below for more than ten minutes when three fellas came among the stock and started saddling up. Nine horses were saddled and I watched as their riders filtered out and forked those nine. Among them were Mexican Bob, on a beautiful sixteen-hand black with a white blaze on his nose and white stockings, and Pedro on a dappled gray. A black fella with gray hair and a fat woman stood and watched them start out plodding down the trail at an easy walk. They watered their mounts in the trickle then sat out at a lope.

Now I had a decision: follow them or take a

closer look at the camp. I chewed on it as I made my way back and decided to work my way back down the ridge and pick up the nine rider's trail. Nine of them all together had to have mischief in mind. They sure as hell weren't going on a picnic.

Gigging the gray to a quick walk, I presumed we were keeping up with the gang...unless they kept up the lope. With the rough country atop the ridge a lope was out of the question. I was near twenty minutes before I could spur into a lope myself, then another few minutes before spotting the road fifty yards ahead. I jerked the gray to a sliding halt, then reined him over into some buck bush as a rider appeared below. I no more than quieted my mount when the rest of the gang appeared, all of them at a quick walk... heading south toward Wickenburg. If that was their destination, we had an eight- or nine-hour ride ahead of us.

The gray and I sat tight giving them time to get at least a half mile ahead, then we followed.

Wickenburg was named for a prospector who made the Vulture Mine gold discovery a few years ago and the town grew up a few miles north where water was more abundant. It missed being the territorial capital by only two votes, but was a thriving community as the Vulture

Mine was one of the most productive in Arizona territory. But I'd heard old man Henry Wickenburg employed a dozen sharpshooters as guards, most of whom had won their fame in the Civil War, and I'm sure even Cade Tolliver and his gang wouldn't try to hit the mine itself. That said I also knew gold had to be shipped and those guards would be split up, some to guard the mine, some the shipment. And the gold was likely locked in the Wickenberg Miner's and Stockman's Bank awaiting a stage to Yuma then south to the Sea of Cortez and ship either around the horn or to the Panama Isthmus and across to the Gulf of Mexico then north to New York.

The hell of it was the Apache, those Crook hadn't rounded up, were fond of stealing the horses and mules from the pack trains and not bashful about taking a few scalps in the process. So, with bandits and Indians, shipping the gold was a risky business...but it had to be shipped, or it was worthless.

I stayed far enough behind the gang to stay out of sight, depending upon the cloud of dust ahead to mark their progress. If the wind disappeared the dust, I slowed to a walk and kept a sharp eye out. The last thing I wanted was to ride close and be seen, and be recognized by Mexican Bob and brother Pedro.

Tate's Station had a fine carved sign and was only a hundred feet off the main road, but it's obvious with no saddle horses at the hitching rail outside that, as Mrs. Johanson had guessed, the Toliver gang had bypassed the place. So, I did as well.

Only a couple of miles more, I passed through a river wash lined with cottonwoods, and spotted a cabin ahead. It was surrounded by a white peeling picket fence, had a substantial garden on one side, a milk cow grazing in a small enclosure on the other, beyond that was an acre of corn and with green about to occlude it, barley or wheat stubble. All this was overseen by an old woman in a rocker on the front porch. She was taking advantage of the cow and churning butter as she rocked. I'm a sucker for buttermilk so couldn't help but inquire. She was not a reckless soul as a double barrel leaned against a porch support in easy reach.

We casually rode the forty yards off the road to near the gate in the fence and I dismounted and called out, "Howdy, ma'am."

She already had the double in hand, aimed my way, and, removing a corn-cob pipe and setting it aside, replied, "Howdy my ass, traveler. What's your business?"

I couldn't help but smile. I didn't often hear a blue-haired octogenarian curse. "Well, ma'am, I was thinking you might take a dime for a glass of buttermilk. Should the churn be in a state to give one up?"

That seemed to soften her resolve. She lowered the scattergun a little. "You with that bunch of rough scum just rode past?"

"No, ma'am. In fact I'm riding careful to keep shy of them."

"You keep short of my gate. I'll fetch a jar and pour you out a fill. You back off and put your dime on a fence post and leave the jar there when you done drunk your fill. If that suits you?"

"Suits me fine, ma'am. You're a careful soul."

"Didn't live this long and stayed this sassy being careless," she said over her shoulder as she disappeared inside, walking cane in one hand, scattergun in the other. When she returned, she was using the scattergun as a walking stick and carrying a jar that would hold a quart. She had some trouble pouring the buttermilk from the churn but managed. She yelled, "Back off twenty paces, leave the dime."

I did so, and she yelled again as she

approached. "Don't you be getting any mischief in mind. My old man's out in the barn and he can notch your ear from a hundred yards with the Sharps he carries."

Stoop shouldered, likely fourscore years old, she managed the gate, traded the dime for the jar, and backed off a few seeming hard-earned steps. Then stood with the scatter gun across her thighs and watched as I gulped down a quarter of the jar.

"What's your business on the road, youngster?" she asked, her brows furrowed in a face already wrinkled and crevassed from years in the sun.

"Traveling to Wickenburg. I'm a smithy and looking for a place to establish my forge."

She studied me a moment while I refreshed my milk mustache and enjoyed the drink.

Then she asked, "We got two mules throwed shoes. Still got the shoes, shaped to fit, and a can full of nails...but the old man has trouble holdin' a hoof and wielding a hammer...should you want to earn that dime back?"

"Ma'am, I'm on the road but if'n we could get right at it...you keep the dime and it'd be my great pleasure to shoe those mules for another glass of buttermilk."

"And I'll throw in a slice of cornbread...in the oven even now."

"Deal," I said. I got a smile from her for the first time. The old lady had all her teeth which was somewhat a surprise as she whistled a little when she spoke, and her faded blue eyes twinkled even as they watered a little.

She advised, "Water your horse out at the barn. Tell the old man I said to feed him a couple of hands full of barley. I ain't walking that far so you yell out plenty loud as you near. He'll be doing whatever old men do to stay away from their old ladies. The old man don't hear so good and it wouldn't do to have you shot while doing us a service."

I matched her smile then fetched the gray. As I led him past where she taken up the churn again, I tipped my hat to her and offered, "I'll yell out every other step. Be back for that cornbread in two shakes of a lamb's tail."

Chapter Twelve

As I was falling behind I took my cornbread with me. I left feeling as if I'd made two new friends. Quincy and Matilda McCalister had cut their little piece of Arizona territory out over ten years ago, which meant they'd fended off Apache and road agents, and had two sons in graves on a hill near the house to prove it. They'd actually been able to file a homestead and claim one hundred and sixty acres, having already proved up the farm and fenced grazing, built an adobe house and plank barn, and brought a spring down from the hill behind in what the Mexicans called a *zanja*, a stone lined ditch, so running water fed barn and a cistern near the house. The water then made its way across the road to pool in the sometimes dry river beyond.

Leaving the McCallister homestead I set off at a lope but even then it was just a few miles shy of Wickenburg before I caught up with the gang, and glad then that they hadn't turned off the road for some other distant target. Hell, for all I knew they were headed for Mexico with their ill-gotten gains. But I thought that unlikely as the ex-slave, Hector, and the fat lady, and who knows who else, were left behind in Dead Mule Canyon. And they dragged no pack animals.

They disappeared from sight while rounding a bend only a quarter mile ahead and I decided to be cautious and reined off to the uphill side of the wagon road to pick my way through the buck-brush, mesquite, and prickly pear cactus for a ways. And it was a good thing I did or I may have passed them not knowing they'd turned off, and ridden into Wickenburg thinking I was still on their tail.

It was probably propitious I heard them before seeing them. They were dismounted and making a small fire for coffee only a hundred yards ahead. I tied the gray to a screwbean mesquite, unsheathed the coach gun—likely in this cover any contest would be close work—and carefully picked my way to within earshot. Other than looking down on the bunch from near their hideout cave, I had yet to get a good look at them. Now I was able to get within seventy-five feet and had a clear view through a couple of voids in the underbrush. I stayed dead still in the shadows and took advantage, almost being discovered by a tall thin bandit with porkchop sideburns and a sombrero even though he looked as Irish as my grandpa. He squatted and did his business not ten paces from me, his back to me, and it was all I could not to close the distance and separate a few vertebra in his neck with the butt of my scattergun.

But that would just alert the rest of them when he was missed and to tell the truth I was curious what nefarious task they'd taken up. As I watched them, I decided to attach my own handles to them. The old boy with the loose bowels I decided to call Porkchop, of course I knew Mexican Bob and brother Pedro. I quickly figured out who Cade Tolliver was as the fellow my tall and maybe even thicker in chest with a two-week stubble bossed the others around. T here were five more. A short thick fella I named Stubby, another no taller and skinny I named Stick, a third looked to be half Indian and who wore a piece of jade in a silver setting around his neck I christened Breed. Somebody had stuck a stick, knife, or finger in his right eye and it had gone pearl white. The fourth had a barrel chest with an abundance of curly blond chest hair and eyes blue as the sky, and a square head. I named the square-head Dutch. And the fifth, with a dozen black warts or moles on his face, was nearly chinless, a nose thin as a blade, lips tight and white as a toad's belly, and generally as ugly as a gila monster...so he got the handle Snake.

So, it was Cade Tolliver, Mexican Bob, Pedro, Porkchop, Stubby, Stick, Breed, Dutch, and Snake on my menu.

After I'd watched them a while and put each ugly mug to memory I faded back into the brush to where I'd tied the gray. He'd about grazed away what he could reach so it was good I'd returned before he started to whinny his displeasure.

They'd gathered up only a hundred yards from the road, and slightly above where it narrowed, not really a cut but with hills rising away on each side. Beyond their campsite, farther from the road, the hill rose even steeper, maybe fifty feet to its crest. I could make my way up a ravine and find a spot on that hill, the high ground, where I could watch their camp, from maybe fifty yards from them and a hundred fifty from the road. I figured it was the road held their interest unless they we just laying up until dark to go on into Wickenburg.

I settled into position, 73 in hand, the gray staked out on the far side of the little rise, me with a decent view of the gang's camp. I'm not there fifteen minutes when I see them saddling up. They move off toward the road and at first I'm ready to run for the gray and follow thinking they're heading out, then I realize they're taking up positions on either side of the road. Looks like another stage robbery.

As they'd likely done for the robbery where Sarah Ann was killed, two of them head on north to make sure traffic doesn't interfere, two of them head south for the same reason, and the other five take up positions, three on one side, two on the other, to intercept and stop the stage.

I'm torn. Do I head for the gray, ride well around them and head the Concord off, or do I use this as an opportunity for my own ends? I decide if they're taking up positions already then there's a good chance I wouldn't be able to intercept the stage nonetheless. The south end of the rise I'm perched on is even closer to the road, so I work my way around until I'm only seventy-five yards from the three on my side of the road, set up so I have a large rock for a rest, and wait.

I don't have to wait long. Hearing the Concord rattling our way, I hunker down and center my sights on the outlaw's back nearest me. It's only moments before the stage appears and I'm surprised by a gunshot from the far side of the road, and the lead mule of the six-up collapses and the stage comes to a stumbling halt.

Recognizing the shotgun guard as the one introduced as Chance I see him stand and pull off a barrel at someone I can't see to his right. And all hell breaks loose as at least two passengers are firing from coach windows. In the first volley, Chance is blown over into the lap of the whip, who I recognize as the fella calls himself Terrill.

While shots are still flying, I pull off on my target and the brother, Pedro, pitches forward in the saddle and his horse carries him away. I take another bead on a rider appearing into the road from the far side and pull off on the big blond outlaw who I'd named Dutch, but it's a hurried shot and I miss, or appear to, as his mount is leaping with the gunfire and he disappears from sight on the far side of the coach, but another appears out of the brush from that side. And I put one into the midsection of the skinny one I'd named Stick. His horse spins and bolts out of under him dumping him on the road. He's kicking like a frog been gigged but I don't believe for long.

The firing has stopped as the whip, Terrill, has about thrown his arms out of joint raising them, and Cade and two other outlaws are looking my way, suspicious of their cohorts being shot and likely knowing no one down below is firing at them. It seems those in the coach have been quieted by the gang's fire. It's my hope the gang will think those I shot, shot each other, or were shot by those in the coach.

Time to take my leave, and I slip off through the brush and head back to the gray. Staying would be inviting seven to come hunting me, and I'm a good one hundred fifty yards from the gray and escape.

To my surprise, I make it without being ridden down, mount up, and move off a hundred yards deep into a thick stand of mesquite and rein up. The stage won't be going anywhere and hopefully those left of the gang will strip all the valuables away and head back to Dead Mule Canyon... without harming other innocents.

It seems I've killed a man.

Maybe two.

It's a small part of the task I've set for myself...even so, I had a wretched taste in my mouth and felt as empty as if I'd been eviscerated. I felt like I'd crossed a rickety bridge with a raging torrent below, and with each step, a plank fell away behind me. There was no going back. It seemed I should cut and run but as the spittle wet my dry mouth again the determination flowed back as well...and seemed to sink deep to the bone marrow. I don't feel much better but I also don't feel a dang bit worse.

I can live with a bad taste a hell of a lot easier than I can live without avenging my beautiful Sarah Ann.

So, I put my mind back to the task at hand. Maybe I can help after they ride out and stay alive to do so.

I'm exhilarated to have gone undetected and to have sent two of the gang to meet their maker...and lived to hopefully drop seven more before my task is done. And not a shot was fired at me. Confidence returns like an avalanche of determination.

I can't help but say aloud, "Sweet Sarah Ann, two down, seven to go."

Chapter Thirteen

I wait until I hear thundering hoofbeats heading north on the road, the gang heading back to Dead Mule Canyon, with any luck. So, I start picking my way back to the crippled coach.

Terrill McNaulty, the whip, has unharnessed the companion to the dead lead horse and is rearranging the six-up harness to become a four up. He's being helped by a buxom woman, so I presume any men passengers have been dispatched. I call out to the whip before I get close.

"Terrill, it's Conn Donahey."

"Come on in. I could use a hand."

I tied the gray off to the boot of the coach and moved forward. Terrill pauses in his work and introduces me. "Conn, this here is Madam Madaline of Wales, England, on her way to Prescott to sing for the folks. Seems she's a bit of a horsewoman and willing to help. Her manager is in the coach, kilt. A drummer, dry goods I believe, is in there dead as well. Was that you I heard shooting."

"It was. Sorry I couldn't do more but there was a whole army of them."

"I don't believe they ever knew there was shooting coming from up the hill. You did good. Nobody else put any lead in them, I'm damn sorry to say. That's a fine lead horse they shot dead and poor Chance here has three fine children all under five years of age." He shook his head in disgust. "And killing our passengers like they was rodents is sure as hell bad for business."

"Like I said, sorry I couldn't do more."

"Them fellas in the coach was already kilt so you did all you could."

"Bullshit." The woman spoke for the first time, second time I'd heard a woman swear. "You could have ridden on down here—"

But Terrill cut her off short. "He could have and more shooting would likely have got you and me killed. You should be thanking him for what he did."

"Humph," she managed. Then added, "I have no interest in riding with a couple of corpses—"

"Three and a wounded man," I corrected.

"No matter," she snapped. "Please put them atop the coach and mop the blood up inside before we continue."

I could see Terrill was getting more than a little irritated. "Ma'am, you can ride atop the coach, you can ride up there aside me, or you can ride inside with them poor dead fellas and who died trying to keep you safe, and with this dead road agent. Your choice, but make it quick as I'm turning back for Wickenburg first flat I come to."

"But...but I have a performance tomorrow in Prescott."

"Afraid you'll be at least a day late."

"My good man—"

"He is a good man," I stopped her short. "And you're alive lady. Were I you I'd be thanking the good Lord and Terrill here for that fact. Maybe you should jerk off a few of them petticoats to mop up the blood?"

"That's arrogant and insulting of you, young man."

"Well, ma'am," I said, "actually it's practical. You got more petticoats than we got shirts."

"Humph," she managed again, then turned to

Terrill. "Help me up in the guard's seat. I'm riding beside you."

The robbers had gone through her bags and fancy duds were spread all over the roadside, so Terrill asked, "You gonna leave your goods here or repack them?"

"I presumed you, representing the express company, would do so."

"Then you presumed wrong, ma'am. They're your goods and not for me to rifle though."

She gave him a "humph" but went about repacking her belongings in three large cases and two smaller ones. Looked to be costumes and hats and such. I never saw so much silk, lace, and feathers.

I looked over to see Pedro's mount, the fat Mexican still in the saddle, moving slowly our way. The rider slumped over the saddle horn doesn't move as the dappled red roan clomps up. I have my Colt in hand and walk over and jerk him out of the saddle and he hits the road on his prodigious belly, puffing out dust, and moaning. He's not dead, but holed, it seems, clean through, aside his belly button. I dearly want to send him to meet his maker, but the woman might take umbrage should I put the muzzle of my Colt in his ear and make a passage through to the other ear.

"You got a piece of rope," I ask Terrill.

"He's gut shot. He ain't gonna live to get back to town."

So, I suggest, hopefully, "Christian thing to do would be put him out of his misery."

"My god," the woman stammered. "You're not suggesting..."

"Ma'am, then how about you help me load him up—"

"I'm not touching that filthy beast."

So, I turn to Terrill. "Guess it's just you and me."

While I rip up Pedro's shirt and stuff his wounds front and back, Terrill digs a lead rope out of the boot and we hog-tie the Mexican on one of the coach seats and mount up. The floor and other seats have bodies stacked like cord-wood. With the off-lead horse trotting free behind, me on the gray leading the Mexican's handsome dappled blue roan, the moaning Mexi-can, the singer's manager, the dry goods drummer, and the dead gang member I've named Stick inside, we set off to find a flat spot to turn the coach around and head back to Wickenburg.

I have no fear going along as I'm sure I know exactly where the Tolliver gang is heading.

As I suspected, and to be truthful, hoped. Pedro was well past breathing by the time we pulled up in front of the Wickenburg-Prescott-Maricopa Wells Express Company office and barns. The Madam was helped down from the shotgun guard's seat and ran for the French Palace Hotel, yelling over her shoulder, "Bring my bags to my room." Terrill watched her go.

He turned to me. "Woman didn't say a damn word all the way back. Didn't shed a tear for her manager."

The City Marshal of Wickenburg strode up. Willis Decker stopped and peeked inside the coach. Then turned to Terrill. "Indians?"

"Willis," Terrill answered with some patience in his voice, "you see any arrows sticking out of the coach or them dead fellows. Cade Tolliver gang had I had my guess."

"They get away with anything?"

"The Vulture Mine box, the freight company box and mail, the personals from a drummer and another fella inside, and from Madam Madaline, who I understand did a concert here night before last. She headed to the French Palace Hotel."

The marshal sighed deeply, then ordered.

"Soon as you're settled here, report to my office. I'll have a secretary there to take your statements." He turned to me. "You lose anything."

"Just a little pride. Wish I could have shot them all."

"Looks like you did fine," he said, and headed off, yelling over his shoulder, "In my office, quick as you can."

Chapter Fourteen

Terrill and I report to the marshal's office, where a young man with quill and parchment awaits to take notes. I'm pleased that after Terrill reports his version of the robbery it had nearly all been said. Still, the marshal turns to me, "Anything to add, young fella?"

I likely should report I know where they're holed up, but I guess it's flat out stingy as I want the pleasure of watching each of them die from Sarah Ann's husband's own hand, so I keep that to myself.

"No, sir. Other than the fact I knew who two of them are. Mexican Bob Comacho and his brother Pedro. Pedro is one of the dead we brought in. Bob is on the run with the rest of 'em.

He's known by a slash of white hair on the right side and a brown sombrero with a band of silver coins. He rides a tall black, maybe a stallion, with a white blaze on his nose and white stockings."

"That's helpful. Anything we can do for you? You may have saved some lives by picking those no-accounts off."

"That's a fine red roan the Mexican rode. You could let me have him and his tack as I could use another mount and one to pack occasionally?"

"Fine by me after we search his saddlebags. Okay with you, Terrill?"

"You bet. We owe this young fella."

The city marshal continued, "There's a two-thousand-dollar flyer out on Tolliver from the governor's office and five hundred dollar out of Maricopa Wells on each of the Comacho brothers—"

Terrill stopped him short. "That's Conn's. He dropped him."

"It'll take a while to get it approved, but when it is your money will be in my safe."

"Take out of it what you think the roan and tack is worth, and I'll pick up the balance."

"Nope, it's all yours and the roan. If you want the Sharps he carried that is worth over twenty and I'll hold that out."

"Hate to ride around with an empty rifle boot," I said, giving him a grin. I've always wanted a Sharps with Pedersoli adjustable sights as it means I can reach out from a long ways off, should I get proficient with it. I'll strip the boot off the roan's saddle and see if I can rig it on a pack saddle.

I'd bet that roan is worth an easy hundred dollars, so it isn't a bad trade, a few .44-40 cartridges for a fine mount and his tack. The fact is, if this hunt drags on, I'll need a pack saddle and paniers and can likely trade the thick-horned Mexican saddle for my requirements. There's a chance this task may take me far from a trading post or cantina.

For the first time, vengeance aside, it dawned on me...this knocking bandits out of the saddle with a chunk of lead and hauling their hides to whomever offers a reward could be a profitable business. It would likely take me five months to earn five hundred at the forge. Of course, the other side of that is the hot forge might be trying to blister me but hunting bandits would be risking a .44-40 in my gullet, and they don't digest well.

I'm returning from the livery with a lead rope and second picket pin, an only slightly used pack saddle, and two bull leather panniers that will hold enough to keep a single fella in grits to last three months when Madam Madaline beckons me from the front porch of the hotel. I doff my hat as I approach.

"Conn, wasn't it?" she asks.

"Yes ma'am, and you'd be Miss Madaline."

"Madam Madaline if you don't mind."

"And why would I mind, ma'am?"

She pauses a moment. I have not taken a fancy to her and I guess it shows.

She sighs a little. "I will pay you one hundred dollars if you'll rent a buggy and drive me to Prescott."

That changes my mind about that shine.

However, I must ask, "You won't be staying for your manager's funeral. I understand they'll bury all those fellas tomorrow."

"Percy O'Toole was a thief and scoundrel. I've paid the five dollars for his burial in a decent pine box...reluctantly. I was going to confront him after the show in Prescott but that's not necessary now."

That makes me smile a little. "I'd guess that goes without saying. A hundred dollars is a lot of money, ma'am. I'm sure a bevy of ol' boys would take on that task for twenty."

"But I don't know those ol' boys and certainly don't know if they'd stand up to outlaws and Indians. I need to go forthwith."

"You pay for the rig's three-day rental in addition and I'll have you in Prescott by dawn if the team holds up, sooner if one of the stage stations will trade stock with me."

"Why three days?" she seems irritated.

"Because I'll lay over a day. Fighting bandits and Indians is hard work." I can't help but laugh a little, then add, "It's sixty miles to Prescott and the team will need to rest and grain up."

I get that "humph" she's getting famous for, but she nods and I'm off.

"I'll have the clerk bring my bags down," she calls after me and I wave over my shoulder.

I nod and head back to the livery where I saw they had a surrey with a roof in case we get a hard rain, with two strong matching blacks as team. We can fill the boot and back seat with her bags if she'll agree to ride up front with me. The gray and the roan are tied to the rear of the surrey. It will be a hard trip and real test for them as I plan to change teams at one of the stage stations along the way. It will be sixty miles for the pair, unless I can board them wherever I trade teams.

She does ride up front without a complaint.

She seems a little irritated that both the coach gun and the 73 are propped between us, that I've paid twelve dollars in advance for the rental, and that there's not room for all her baggage in the boot so the back seat is taken up as well. The gray's saddle and the roan's pack saddle helps fill the space to overflowing. I presume she meant to flop down and catch some sleep. Madam Madaline is a handsome woman but hard to coax a smile from, middle-aged, buxom, well-dressed in a city sort of way. I do admire her smelling like lilacs, her tenacious way, and her willingness to withstand some hardships to fulfill her obligations.

We had more than nine hours of daylight left as it wasn't getting dark until eight p.m., so I took full advantage of it, alternating between a walk and a trot or even cantor. I was surprised when Madam Madaline didn't complain as the road had plenty of bumps and bounces and the faster pace accentuated them. She was tougher than she looked. It wasn't long before she unpinned the wide-brimmed bonnet she wore and removed it before it blew off.

We stopped at Tate's Station where I thought of changing horses but the blacks were only slightly lathered and I figured them good for another fifteen miles. Myrtle Mae Tate did sell us each a glass of sun tea for a dime and we were glad to pay it. She tried to sell us a lunch of beans and biscuits but my employer wanted to move on so we took a couple of biscuits slathered in what the lady called Tuna Jelly, made from prickly pears, and it suited us fine, washed down with some water from a jug the livery had provided.

It was dusk when I reined up at the Skull Valley Trading Post and made a deal with Gusav Johanson to trade the blacks for a couple of skunk-stripped dun mules, with the understanding we'd trade back in a couple of days. He also agreed to stall and grain the gray and the roan. The old bandit charged us two dollars for the rental plus a dollar a day for the riding and pack horse. I tucked it in the back of my mind to add that to the insult of allowing Mexican Bob and Pedro to run free. I didn't mention to him that I'd shot straight enough to blow a hole in brother Pedro's fat gut and earned myself five hundred in the process.

When I needed no more favors from Gustav I'd rub his nose in that one. Had it not been for Gustav insisting they go free, at the point of a firearm, I likely wouldn't have had the pleasure of watching Pedro die, as I'd likely have delivered him live to the Yavapai Sheriff. So maybe I owe Gustav as he unknowingly did me a favor.

Anna Gustav, now one of my favorite people, unlike her husband, sold us a slice of apple pie which would serve as supper and we were quickly back on the road. The mules were well broken but didn't favor the lope or cantor as the blacks did, but they were sure-footed and constant and kept up a fast walk. Luckily the moon was near full if waning, and sure-footed and more sure of themselves than horseflesh was a good thing in the dark moon-shadow-laced trail. We clomped into town, the mules and us bone tired. I knew Joseph Ehle slightly, the proprietor of the new Montezuma Hotel, but didn't take the risk of ringing the bell and awaking whoever might be on duty. I slipped around behind the desk and found a key to the President's Suite—my employer said it had been promised to her—and with three trips hauled Madam Madaline's bags to the second-floor rooms. The corner rooms overlooked Montezuma and Willis streets and offered an easy walk to anywhere of any merit. The Madam retired to her sleeping room and dug five twenty-dollar gold pieces and the price of the surrey rental out of a money belt she confided she wore and handed them over with a sincere smile.

I was becoming a man of means again. I could cement that situation by recovering the proceeds of the sale of Fenton's from the Cade Tolliver gang.

And I wouldn't rest until I did so and afterward threw dirt in their faces.

Chapter Fifteen

To my surprise and pleasure Madam Madaline promised two tickets would be waiting at the door for her performance, only fifteen hours hence. I couldn't help but get a little choke in my throat wishing Sarah Ann was here to attend with me. Which put my attention back to my task at hand, and my jaw clamped. I headed for Alleandro's, let myself in, and stalled the mules and found a soft spot in the hay for myself. I'd settle up with him when sunlight washed the streets of Prescott.

I'd guess it took to about the count of three before I was to snoring.

Alleandro woke me moving some horses around and seemed happy I was back and back whole. I paid him a dollar for the night and invited him to attend Madam Madaline's concert as my guest and he seemed tickled to accept and informed me the next night's lodging for me and the mules would be on him. Kindness repaid.

Then I headed for Ma Hoyts as my stomach was flapping against my backbone.

I was surprised to be congratulated by a couple of fellows on the street for the capture-killing of Pedro Comacho. Then realized the telegraph ran from Wickenburg to join up with the line from Fort Whipple to Yuma and on to San Diego...and thanks to the Army news now flew around the territory. But it wasn't cheap, telegraphic communication for the general public cost: From Prescott to San Diego, $1.50 for 10 words; to Yuma $1.25; Tucson $1.25, Florence $1.00; Maricopa Wells $1.00, Phoenix $1.00 and Wickenburg $0.75. For each additional five words, the rate was 75 cents. It was possible for citizens to communicate instantly from distant locales. I was even more surprised to pick up the restaurant's paper, the morning's issue of the *Miner*, on entering and see a nearly still wet paper with a front-page article, above the fold, about the latest robbery of the Prescott-Wickenburg-Maricopa Wells Concord, the killing of the shotgun guard and two passengers, and the slaying of the robber

Pedro Comacho and an unknown accomplice by a passerby, one Conn Murphy Donahey, recently of Prescott.

A couple of local businessmen who knew me from Fenton's Forge gave me a pat on the back and bought me breakfast.

All this was fine, except I'm sure the news traveled quickly to Cade Tolliver and gang and I was now on top the list of scalps to hang among the folderol on their saddles—particularly that of the well-known killer Mexican Bob, also known as Roberto Comacho, and known to trade coats with Cade Tolliver himself. So, I cussed the telegraph wire and the *Miner*. There are times when one's accomplishments are best left hidden away.

Somewhat surprised, I also learned from the paper I'd been in the company and the employee of fame. It seemed, even though I paid little attention to such matters, that Madam Madaline was a European trained singer of great repute and had only recently arrived in the territories from performing in Boston, New York City and the countries birthplace, Philadelphia, to grace the populace of the hinterlands with her talents.

I spent the day in the plaza, in the shade of the magnificent new courthouse, playing dominos and throwing horseshoes and was proud to have only donated two dollars to all the old one arm and one leg Civil War vets passing their days there.

Before meeting up with Alleandro I stopped by the Palace, visited with bartender Alexis and dealer Doc Holliday, and was happy to buy both he and Virgil Earp three fingers of the finest and to receive their congrats for ridding the territory of Pedro Comacho.

"Rifle or handgun," Holliday asked.

"73, from near a hundred yards," I answered. "And no cheap tricks with a shotgun."

"Good," he gave me a tight smile. "I don't place much faith with the shotgun, don't want to face off at fifty yards and trust the load, but to each his own. Fact is, most of those louts couldn't hit their ass with both hands much less a man at one hundred yards even with a Winchester. Nonetheless, there are times you can't account for your bad luck and their good...next time make it a hundred twenty."

"Yes, sir," I said, and returned his smile with a grin.

Then he added. "You're a wise young man not to boast. In matters of gun fighting boasting will only draw those who want to build their reputation on outgunning others, even if it be back-shooting."

I gave him a nod and he went back to dealing faro.

True to her word Madam Madaline left us two tickets at the doorway and it was a good thing as the three-dollar seats were sold out. I could now understand why the one-hundred-dollar payment was no problem for her. With the tickets was a note to me, "Join me in my dressing room after the show. We have things to discuss." Even accompanied by a local on the piano, another on a violin, and a third on a flute—none of them professionals—she bowled the crowd over with renditions of *Camptown Races, Carry Me Back to Old Virginny, Marguerite,* and a dozen others before finishing off with *Libiamo ne'lieti calici—Verdi,* composer. Verdi's rousing 'Drinking Song' from his much-loved opera *La traviata* is what's known as a *brindisi,* a lively song that encourages the consumption of wine. I would not have known a lick of that had not a flyer been passed among the crowd explaining to us bumpkins the Italian. Even not understanding, the crowd remained dead silent until giving her a thunderous ovation that I'm surprised didn't cave in the place.

She was called back for three curtain calls before the manager came on and said she must retire.

I excused myself from Alleandro's company to join her, much to his dismay as he was not invited, but with the promise I'd join him in the Palace and buy him a beer.

To my great surprise when I showed the note to the backstage guard and he escorted me to her dressing room, not fancy but only enclosed by curtains, she rose and walked to me and gave me a nice hug and peck on the cheek, then seated me on a stool next to hers. It took a moment for the blush and heat to fade from my cheeks.

She wasted no time, "I'm in need of a manager and to be truthful a bodyguard, and I'd like to offer you—"

"Madam, I have a task at hand. One my heart and soul says I must complete."

"Monsieur Vendame, the owner here, told me of the death of your beautiful wife—"

Again, I interrupted. "I'm so very complimented, but this is a matter of the heart and hot lead, and I won't be discouraged or dissuaded. It's something I must do or I'll not be able to live with myself." Were both silent for a moment until I continued. "And the fact is you wouldn't want me as an employee, particularly a bodyguard, if my mind was elsewhere."

I merely shook my head.

She continued, "Have you seen Shakespeare's play *Romeo and Juliet*? A love story with lots of violence...and it ends badly for both of them."

"I believe I'll do my best to write my own ending, ma'am. So, sorry but I must decline."

"Not even for one hundred and twenty-five dollars a month."

I give her a sad smile. "Not for a thousand dollars a month."

She rose, which was a signal for me to do so also, and walked me to the split in the curtains. "Conn, should you finish your task, and if God wills you to live through it, my next stop is in Denver, then Cheyenne, then I'll be taking the Transcontinental to San Francisco. If you're ready to take a job...it may not be as manager, but I'll have a job for you. Wire me and I'll send you transportation money."

I felt a little maudlin as I headed for the Palace. So down in the mouth I had only one beer with Alleandro then saw Rafe, Randolph, Duncan and Murdoch Macintosh stride in and decided a retreat was in order.

Besides, I wanted to be fresh as I was headed

back to Mule Canyon with the dawn. I had high hopes I'd find someone to return the surrey to Wickenburg, otherwise it was an extra fifty-mile round trip, thirty from the Skunk Valley Trading Post to Wickenburg then more than twenty back to Dead Mule Canyon.

I was back at Alleandro's Livery before my normal sack time so I carefully cleaned and reloaded my firearms and checked my other weapons. I only had a half dozen shells for the .45-90 Sharps, but had reloading gear should I need more. I had four boxes of fifty for the .44-40 Colt's and 73, which were interchangeable, and four boxes of twenty-five for the coach gun: one of 7 shot if I needed to bird or small game hunt, one of single balls which would down a man or deer inside a hundred yards, and two of double ought buck—each shell loaded with nine pellets each equal to a .32, in case I needed to clear out a saloon...or cave.

Not to speak of a bear trap that would likely take a man's foot off should he make the mistake of sneaking up on me along the line where I might place it.

Add four cans of one-half pound each of black powder, the detonators, and ten feet of fuse to turn their placement into fiery hell.

I slept well, knowing I was ready.

Chapter Sixteen

I had harness on the mules before the sun colored the eastern sky and we sat out an easy trot, as I'd yet to wet my throat I stopped at the Iron Springs Trading Post, which also served as the stage station, and was just in time for Martha McNab's fine biscuits and coffee that would float a spoon. As I ate and visited with Martha, Chauncey watered my mules then had a six-up ready for the incoming stage. Terrill McNaulty passed me with a wave, not four miles past Iron Springs. He was back working the whip, with a new fella sitting shotgun, another guard riding on top with a rifle in hand and a coach gun in easy reach. Seem's the express company was upping their security...and a stage full of passengers. Six filled the coach and two rode atop with the second guard. Both of them carried long arms. I truly hoped I wouldn't come upon them all shot to hell somewhere down the road. The other side of that coin was Cade Tolliver might reckon the opposition was getting to risky and light out for parts distant.

The first half of the trip was uneventful until I reined up short of the Skull Valley Trading Post and Express Station. Four horses adorned the hitching rail. But I had no choice as Gustav was boarding my gray, roan and the surrey blacks. I tied the team off aside the four and pocketed two double ought buck shells in each trouser pocket, made sure the double was loaded, checked the loads in my Colt and slipped a pea in the sixth chamber—I normally didn't carry one under the hammer—then walked around to come in, unexpected I hoped, the back way.

I took a deep calming breath, cocked both barrels, and pushed through. Anna Johanson looked up, a little surprised and waved but I was scanning the room. Elena was helping a customer and three others were spotted around the post, none of them armed, none of them looked anything like the brigands I hunted. I relaxed and let the hammers down, and only then returned Anna's greeting.

"Conn, I just made a pitcher of lemonade?"

"Love some, thank you, ma'am."

I took the stool nearest the cash box as Elena arrived there with the customer. She greeted me with a dazzling smile, "Conn, you're back, and healthy. We heard of your exploits."

"Heard from Mexican Bob, I suppose?"

That took her aback for a moment. "We haven't seen that bunch since you were last in. A traveler dropped off a copy of the *Miner*."

I turned to her gray-haired customer who was paying Anna for his supplies. "May I ask, sir, where are you bound?"

"You may. No secrets here. Wickenburg then on to the Vulture Mine. We heard they are hiring."

"I don't suppose you'd like to go in style and earn a dollar for your ease of travel?"

"Explain."

"I have a rig outside needs returning to the livery in Wickenburg. I'll pay you a dollar for your trouble...not that it's trouble to ride under cover out of the sun with a *compadre* by your side should you desire."

He laughed. "Sounds like I should be paying you. Damn rights I'll drive it on in."

I stuck out my hand. "Conn Donahey."

"Albert Sturges," he said, "friends call me Al," and shook.

Gustav entered the back door and I figured I'd better make sure my animals were fine, and asked, "How's the gray and roan doing?"

"And good day to you, Conn. They are better than when you left them and yours again for two dollars."

I handed him his fee and asked, "Please harness up the blacks and recover your mules. As you can see they are at least as sound as when we traded."

I nodded, dug in my pocket and came up with four two-bit pieces and handed them over to Albert Sturges. "I'm trusting you with a fine team of blacks and a beautiful surrey. Just so's you know, I've been known to ride five hundred miles to right a wrong, so don't take on this job unless you mean to finish it honestly."

Albert gave me a steely gaze. "Young fella, I never did a crime in all my fifty years and sure as hell," he turned to Martha and Elena, "pardon my language, ladies." Then back to me. "Sure ain't gonna start now. You doubt me you can put this dollar where the sun don't shine."

That got a smile out of me. "I am convinced, sir. I need to grab a set of saddlebags out of the surrey."

"Surrey." He smiled. "I figured some old farm wagon. This'll be a real pleasure."

I treated Al and his three friends to a lemonade while Gustav switched out the teams.

Soon, Albert and one of his traveling mates tied off their saddle horses to the surrey and set out with grins.

As I was finishing my lemonade I questioned the beautiful Elena, "Mexican Bob hasn't been back?"

Her demeanor turned serious. "To be truthful, I told him I would never consider more than waiting on him here at the post. He did not take that news well and I don't think he departed thinking us even friends, much less more." Then she added, "If you see Bob he will avenge his brother, and even if you don't see him, watch your back. He has no honor."

I nodded, then changed the subject and engaged her in what I hoped was a pleasant conversation. We talked of her birth in Hermosillo, her family's migration to Arizona territory, and the farm they lost, on the banks of the Gila River after the Apache killed her ma and pa and burned the lean-to and barns her papa had built. She'd survived hidden in a root cellar beneath a pile of rotting potatoes and lived off them until being discovered the Johansons. I'd figured her for half-white and was surprised when she said both parents Mexican. But then I've seen Mexicans near blond and blue-eyed.

The Johanson's came along with a wagon train bound for Yuma then California, but seeing what the Apache had done left the train, took an eleven-year-old Elena with them, and headed north hoping to go to Prescott. They came upon a spot with decent creek bottom soil and a good spring, now a trading post, and settled there, soon to be offered a job as express station as they were fifteen miles north of Wickenburg on the stage road.

I was in no rush to ride to the cave. I planned to stay on the south rim of the canyon this time so I could look down on the face of the cave. Darkness would be my friend and a light sky would mean I would be sky-lined, even if only for a short time.

Likely I could tell the number of occupants from the number of horses in their remuda. I did know there was, or had been, Cedric the black former slave, and the near obese woman, in residence. Whatever course of action I decided to take, I did not want to harm innocents. That would make me no better than those I hunted.

I decided to leave the roan, most my camp gear, and the Sharps with Gustav and packed the gray with my bedroll, the 73 in a boot on one side and the coach gun in a boot on the other. Resting a while in Gustav's barn I waited until the setting sun was its own width over the mountains to the west and set out. By the time I turned up Dead Mule Canyon it had dipped below the rim. Where the canyon split it was an easy climb up the middle ridge and only a half mile to where, with only a three-quarter waning moon for light, I could look down on the face of the cave, maybe one hundred fifty yards to the south.

Coming to the edge of the pines just as it was truly dark, I found a flat and dismounted and picketed the gray and made my way south until a rocky escarpment fell away and I had a clear view. There was a campfire going twenty yards from the cave entrance, it a hole some twenty feet high and no more than ten wide. Light poured from it so another campfire must burn inside, or possibly a couple of coal oil lanterns.

The fat woman tended a big Dutch oven hanging from a tripod of running irons over the fire and only steps away someone with masonry skills had constructed a stone oven and a small fire glowed in the fire hole below the oven which appeared to have a metal door. Only a dozen paces from there was a trickle of water. It was a fine camp, presuming the cave itself was habitable, and would work summer or winter.

As I studied the scene a man walked out of the cave into the firelight and fetched a pile of tin bowls and spoons and an iron hook. He set aside the Dutch oven lid with the hook then ladled something into the bowls, stew I presume, and he and the woman carried them inside, making two trips and they finally disappeared inside for good. It was another quarter hour before one of the gang wandered out and downstream to find a spot where they'd placed a six inch log between two rocks so a fella could set there upon and hang over for his necessary. I presume they'd dug a hole behind. I could not make out who the fella tending his personal business was, as it was just too dang dark. But I'd seen enough.

My next question was if there was another exit from the cave. I decided I'd never know, so didn't worry about it.

As the cooking chores, and horse and mule remuda chores, seemed to fall to the former slave and the fat woman, I was in hopes of talking with him to see where his loyalty holed up. I was not comfortable with he and the woman being caught up in my retribution plans.

Chapter Seventeen

I had a hunch the black, Hector, would be the first to check on the horses come morning, so I had hopes of catching him there, forty paces or so from the cave. The corral was backed by some tall buckbrush and the beginning of scrub pines.

Rising before dawn, I saddled up and rode the ridge until I was a quarter mile up the canyon then picked my way along until I found a well-traveled game trail leading down and let the gray choose his way to the bottom. We both watered up at a pool with what appeared to be the spring that fed the trickle that passed on by the cave. There was no water above the pool. Then we turned that way and when I figured I was forty yards or so up canyon from the remuda, tied off the gray where we could make a fast retreat, carried the coach gun, and slipped through the brush as quiet as possible.

Sure as hell just as the sky began to turn gold behind me, me hidden in the brush behind the rails of the corral holding their stock, I saw someone making their way out of the cave. I soon recognized it to be Hector, his gray hair lit by a sliver of sun now just above the mountains behind. Unfortunately, just as he reached the rails, another fella exited the cave and walked away from the opening. Luckily he went downstream away from my hideout, and let his own stream fly into the brush.

Hector carried four lead ropes and neck tied four animals and led them out to water. By the time he returned the other owlhoot shook it off and wandered back to the cave.

The rails nearest the cave were lined with saddles, blankets, saddlebags, and bridles and when Hector returned he left the four he'd taken to water with lead ropes and tied them off to the top rail and began saddling. Before he could pull cinch on the first I moved into the corral and among the other eight horses there until I was only fifteen feet from him, and gave him a low whistle. He turned and as he was now staring into the sun, shaded his eyes with a hand.

"Hector, move over this way," I said in a low voice.

"Who dat?" he asked, taking only a couple of steps my way.

"A friend. Anna Johanson sent me."

"Mrs. Anna?"

"Come on over. I don't want to be heard."

I guess hearing Anna's name convinced him I was not a threat, and he moved over. I was talking over a buckskin-colored horse and he kept him between us so we palavered over his back. The buckskin was fine with me leaning on him and I rubbed his withers as I rested there.

As soon as Hector arrived, concerned, he looked back over his shoulder before he asked, "You da law?"

"No, sir, Conn Donahey, but I'm no friend of those inside. They murdered my wife. But...I don't want to see you or the woman hurt so I'm giving you a chance to stay out of the way."

"Señora Sanchez is Mexican Bob's aunt. She's as damn mean as the others."

"You then. You're saddling up those four."

"Tolliver, Bob, Carlos Apaza, and Shorty McFearson are riding out and all the way to the

Vulture Mine and to a couple of other new claims. Lookin' to make another score, they call it. Re... recon...reconnoiter, Mr. Cade calls it. What you got in mind?"

"First, why haven't you run off? You've been a free man for more than ten years."

"Mr. Tolliver pays me a dollar a day and found. I ain't got nowhere to go and I been with the Tolliver family since I was a welp."

"Then you're loyal to him? How come you're talking with me?"

"I hate dat son of a bitch. He and his black-hearted daddy sold my wife and son off during the war to a no-good with a careless cat-o'-nine-tails, and they died in cannon fire on the plantation next to the Tollivers—"

"Then why stay?"

"Where de devil was I to go? I don't do no robbin' and killin' yet there be flyers out on me right along with the rest of them. Some bounty man likely drag me off to jail and most town folk say I was guilty just for being a black man. And should I try and ride off there ain't nobody could outride boss Tolliver and Mexican Bob. Last fella tried to leave the gang, Bob lassoed him and dragged him down the river bouncin' his head off dem rocks till he drowned'ed like a barn rat."

That made some sense to me. I cleared my throat before I asked, "They got lots of other people's money in that cave, I bet?"

"There's a chest in there could only be carried by a stout farm wagon...but Mr. Cade always has two neck saddlebags each half full of gold bars and coins and the rest stuffed with paper money wherever he goes, and that chest is locked tight wit a padlock big'er than my fist."

Somebody yelled from the mouth of the cave. "Where the hell are them horses?"

"Comin' boss," Hector yell over his shoulder.

I lowered my voice. "When you hear a rock roll down just outside the cave, you got about one minute to get the hell out of there. As soon as you're out of sight of the others, you run lickity-split until the rocks and dust settles behind you."

"You gonna—"

"Is there another way out of the cave?"

"Hector!" the yell came again.

"Don't know, don't never go back there, there's bats and such." He turned back toward the voice. "Comin' boss," he yelled over his shoulder.

"In a couple of hours, you get ready to get the hell out of the way," I said as he went back to saddling.

Just as I slipped out of the corral and back

into the brush, I heard that same voice yell, "You Ethiopian son of a bitch, what the hell you been doing? I'll beat you to mush."

"Sorry boss, I had to take care of my bowels. That *Tia* Sanchez put too damn many peppers in dem beans."

"Ten minutes and we better be ready to ride out."

"Yes, boss, yes sur, ten minutes."

He turned back but I was already deep in the underbrush.

The gray and I kept moving quiet and picked our way. By the time I rode the ridge back and was due south of the cave it was full light. I tied the gray off and busted brush to the edge and was just in time to see Cade Tolliver, Mexican Bob, the one I'd named Breed, and the one I'd named Stubby, riding out down the canyon. I'd made a mental note, Hector said Carlos Apaza and Shorty McFearson. I hope the nicknames were descriptive as one was truly slim and the other short.

Tolliver was mounted on a beautiful animal with a blond mane and tail and chocolate body, a chestnut I'd call him, with a mane a foot long and a tail nearly dragging the ground. I made note of that as it was an animal I'd spot among a hundred.

Again, they had no pack animals, so I was sure they were returning to the cave, and I had other business at the moment. I let them get far ahead then found a game trail and crossed over.

When I got even with where I knew the cave to be I left the gray cinched and staked him near enough graze he'd be content for an hour. Removing one one-pound can of black powder, a Hercules detonator, and cutting off two feet of fuse I worked my way to a ledge of rock over cave entrance. The ledge had a three-foot-deep cleft I could edge the can into which would assure the charge would blow plenty of rock away. The entrance was probably seventy-five feet below. Working the detonator into the can of powder, I fixed the fuse in place, pulled a box of lucifers out of my shirt pocket and moved closer to the entrance. I'd promised Hector a warning so I picked up a medium boulder of eight inches and heaved it so it would bounce over the edge. I could see it knocked a couple of others over as well so it was a minuscule landslide as compared with what was to come.

I lowered the powder can into the cut and used a small branch to push it down firmly in place. Then I started a count. Knowing the fuse was good for about thirty seconds for every six inches—I'd watched my old man remove many a stump by setting charges—I counted a full minute, then struck the lucifer and lit the fuse. I hoped this fuse was equal to that my old man had used, and hoped Hector got the signal of falling rocks. In a little less than two minutes I'd have an answer to both questions.

I ran for the gray, jerked the picket pin, swung into the saddle and gave him my heels. He must have sensed my urgency as he damn near leaped out from under me.

Chapter Eighteen

I was near a hundred yards back toward the main road when the shock of the explosion whacked me in the back and made the gray take five energetic leaps forward before I calmed him. I reined him to the north on the first game trail presented itself, found the canyon bottom and the trickle of water, let him have his fill then started back up canyon to see what damage I'd done. Likely there were four still inside who'd breathed their last, if the fat woman Hector said was as evil as the rest was there. Hopefully Hector had gotten my signal and gotten well clear.

I didn't want to hurt Hector, and it galled me to hurt a woman, even an evil one, but as my pa always said, you lie down with dogs you're gonna get fleas. In this case, you run with murdering scum, you're likely to reap what you sow...or they sow.

Sure of one thing I couldn't help but smile, whatever ill-gotten gains they had, other than what they may carry, was likely safely buried under tons of granite.

As I approached it was clear Hector was sitting pretty, perched on an escarpment of rocks that rose nearly to the top of the cave opening. I slowed the gray walk. There was more than a foot of clearance atop the fallen rock, enough a man could crawl out if he was still able to crawl. It was more than a little surprising to see the woman perched on a round boulder at the bottom of the rockfall. Either Hector had a change of heart regarding her evilness, or just had a touch of "I can't harm a woman" as did I.

He yelled out to me as I got within forty yards, "You said it be Conn, right?"

"Conn it is." I kept plodding forward and reined up only ten feet from where the woman sat, her butt an axe handle wide hanging over the rock on each side, her arms as big as my thighs, and her glare as mean as a teased rattler.

I dismounted and as I did so, she came up with a little belly gun that almost disappeared in her hand and pulled one off. It took me in the meat on my left shoulder just as my right foot hit the ground. This time I was glad the gray shied as I still had my left foot in the stirrup and he spun away and ran twenty yards with me hanging on like a remora on a shark. She pulled off the second barrel, missed both me and the gray, or so I hoped, and I pulled the 73 and slapped the gray's rump and he trotted off. My arm was operable enough for me to hoist the rifle as she waddled to where a Starr breech loader leaned against the rock.

I yelled at her, "Don't do it. You won't make it."

Guessing she thought me more a gentleman than I'd come to be over the last month, she grabbed it up.

My .44-40 didn't care if she was of the female persuasion or not, particularly with a generous amount of blood dripping off my elbow. I barely felt the kick or realized I'd pulled the trigger...and as she rolled backward over the same rock the Starr had leaned on blood flared from between her watermelon breasts, marking the dirty white blouse she wore, and her eyes rolled back in her head. She was so fat she didn't really fall, rather kind of rolled until her legs poked up in the air from behind the boulder.

Standing there in a bit of shock, I realized I'd just killed a woman.

Thank God one who'd already shot me and wanted to finish the job, but still a woman. I examined the flesh wound on my left shoulder, jerked my neckerchief from around my neck, and applied pressure.

Hector walked over to where her fat legs stuck up in the air and stared down at her, then glanced back at me. "Her nickname was Bruja 'cause she fancied herself a witch...*bruja* is witch in Mexican. You done did the world a favor, young Conn. I do believe the good Lord cast this one aside long ago. Some say Lord Jesus don't give up on no one, but I don't believe even Jesus could condone this foul-mouthed daughter of the devil."

I sighed and took a deep calming breath. His words did little to fill the void in my gut. "I feel a mite empty inside...then again I guess I had no choice. That Starr is likely .54 caliber and woulda blown a hole in me bigger than your fist."

"Like I said, you done did the world a favor. Best we bind that shoulder."

I motioned up at the top of the escarpment. "First, any squawking from the cave?"

"Nary a whisper so far."

Hector and I both stood quiet and listened, hearing nothing but the trickle of water in the little stream and the nicker of horses and mules.

I asked him, "Who was in the cave?"

"Choctaw, Billy Bob Ten Gauge and Wichita. No idea their real names."

The gray had stopped at the remuda to nose to nose with the horses and mules there so I moved over and untied his lead rope from the saddle ties and tied him to the top rail, then returned to Hector who had ripped some of her full skirt away.

He held a bottle of pulque in one hand and poured it on my wound. I tried not to flinch but it stung like hell. He handed me the bottle so I could take a swig but I refused with a "thank you."

"Will it stitch up?" I asked.

"Went clean through, hole front and back. Don't think it even nicked the bone. I guess a fair hand with a needle might close them holes somewhat."

I nodded. "You got a shovel?"

"I do, gonna take a hell of a hole for his one."

I thought it impolite to smile so quelled the upturned lips. "Suggest you get her planted and at least covered with rocks so the critters don't have at her. I'm riding down to the trading post to see if the ladies there might put a needle to this, then I suggest you join up and we ride into Prescott and I'll stand up for you with the sheriff and maybe we can get those flyers with your name taken down."

He's silent for a moment, then shook his head. "Young sir, I do believe they'll hang me."

"Was it truthful when you said you'd robbed or killed no one?"

"Never harmed no one in all my days."

"I have a bit of a name there and have come to know Marshal Vigil Earp and Sheriff Beaumont, and believe my word carries some weight. I will stand up for you."

"Or maybe cut me down and throw dirt on my box?"

"Only if you're not being truthful with me? You don't clear this up you'll be looking over your shoulder the rest of your days and when they catch up with you and they will...likely you'll not have me near to stand up beside you."

He's silent for a long moment, then nods. "At your word, sur." He moved away to a rack with shovel, hoe, pick, and axe. Then turned back to me. "You get on to them ladies with the needles. I'll be along soon enough."

"I do believe that's a wise decision. We'll ride on into Prescott and we'll go see Sheriff Beaumont together."

"Yes, sur. And I believe I'll start the praying right now."

I was still leaking blood from the wound, front and back, when I stumbled into see Elena behind the counter. She ran to me and led me out the back and across the yard to the house. As she sat me at a kitchen table, she yelled for her ma, Anna, who came running. They unwrapped and eyed the wound.

"Gunshot?" Anna asked.

"Yes, ma'am," I replied.

Gustav stomped in. "I told you, young Conn. Firearms lead only to bloodshed."

I ignored him, wanting to reply, "they ain't for pounding nails" but kept my mouth shut as Anna sent Elena for her sewing box. She then turned to Gustav and with a sharp voice, insisted, "We'll be busy here. You go watch the post."

He nodded and minded.

Elena returned and Anna got prepared then handed me a wooden spoon. "Good thing this was a small caliber. Bite down on that, Conn. This will smart a little."

Dang if she wasn't right.

But with the beautiful Elena looking on I sure as hell wasn't going to whine. I didn't hardly even flinch. However, I did leave teeth marks in her spoon.

Chapter Nineteen

Hector arrived with eight head of horses and four mules. He must be a good hand with stock as six of them were tail-tied, from neck of one to tail of the one in front. Five he let run free knowing they'd stay with the herd. The lead mare he rode. He'd left all the tack but that on the skunk-stripped dun he rode and Gustav squealed like a stuck hog when Hector suggested they be boarded and Cade Tolliver billed when he returned.

Gustav at first refused saying it wasn't Tolliver asking to board the stock, until Hector said he'd drive them back, corral them, and leave a note Gustav refused them and if they were starved it was on Gustav. The stage station owner then decided he'd take his chances being paid by

Tolliver which was better than taking his chances being shot by Tolliver.

I could have driven them on into Prescott and turned them over to Sheriff Beaumont as assets confiscated from the robber band but my arm was paining me and it would have taken extra time, and I felt obligated to get the matter of Hector settled with Sheriff Beaumont.

It was early morning before we got to the sheriff's office and he was nowhere to be found so I took Hector to Ma Hoyt's for breakfast. We'd talked the whole way in from Skunk Valley and I found myself particularly happy for trying to help the man. He was in his late forties but didn't know his birthday, he'd never learned to read or write, but was a hand and skilled with every chore on a farm and with stock. He'd known only the Tollivers from the time he was born, and from listening to his stories I found them a piss poor example of Christian folks. My family had never owned slaves and my pa was an abolitionist and served his time in the Union as a cooper and wheelwright. He came home in one piece only to die of cholera.

Prescott was about equal folks who fought with north or south, but it was apparent those who had put the war behind them as when we walked into Ma Hoyt's I could hear the comments from some nearby tables, and they weren't complimentary.

In fact two big louts, probably miners, at the table next to the one we took stopped Ma's daughter, Juanita, as she passed with coffeepot in hand, and the one with his hand on her arm growled, "You gonna let that darky eat in here?"

Juanita shook his hand off and took three steps and leaned down and put her arm alongside Hector's and turned back to the big miner. "Aww, as I suspected. I am as dark as this gentleman. So, you don't want him fed and you don't want me to serve you? Maybe you don't want mama to cook for you?"

The two dug into dirty canvas trousers, dropped some coins on the table, and rose and stomped out.

I laughed. But as Juanita left to turn in our order, Hector eyed me. "You think I get a fair shake in dis town? 'Bout as likely as me gettin' elected mayor. Maybe I jus' keep on moving down the trail."

Eyeing him a long moment I couldn't help but repeat, "And you'll have a sore neck the rest of your days from lookin' back. Seems like the law will be after you and likely Cade Tolliver and party won't think kindly on you leaving Tia Sanchez in a shallow grave and his pards under tons of rock."

He gave me an argument hard to dispute. "He and the law likely think I'm under there too."

"There is that," I replied, "and I won't say different. Your call, Hector. But the folks at the Skunk Post did see you and you did leave him a note. Maybe that was a mistake?"

We ate in silence, then I guess I'd convinced him I was truly on his side as he mopped his mouth and suggested, "You done? Let's go see dat sheriff. Maybe he back."

"Fine idea," and we headed out.

As we walked along Hector turned to me and surprised me. "You know, on the plantation we done took the name of them what owned us. But Tolliver sticks in my throat when I say it and makes my brain go hot when I think it. Were I to take the name Donahey would it offend?"

I had to laugh, then suggest, "Hell, Hector, I'd be proud to have you as a brother what I know of you to date. Besides, I ain't the only Donahey in creation. You could take Abraham Lincoln for all it is to me. No, sir, no problem with this Donahey."

He merely nodded, then added, "Then Hector Donahey it is."

I laughed again. "Not sure I'd claim Irish how-some-ever."

At that he laughed too.

We entered the sheriff's office to find him behind his desk ruffling through a pile of papers. Across from him sat two fellas I knew to be deputies. They rose and offered us their chairs. We didn't sit until Beaumont waved us down.

"What's your business?" he asked.

Hector sat quiet as I began, "Need to clear up some misunderstandings."

We were there a good hour as I acted attorney for the defense and Hector mostly sat quiet, except for telling all he knew about the Cade Tolliver gang and offering to repeat it again at a deposition. He also promised to get a job in Prescott and not leave until the Tolliver gang was brought to trial and he testified.

From there we walked to Alleandro's and I soon had him employed after assuring my friend that Hector knew stock and knew how to work.

We parted with a handshake and I mounted the gray, and against Sheriff Beaumont's wishes, headed back south.

My shoulder was paining me but healing and

not weeping blood. If I lived through this quest, I'd have a puckered scar across the back of my neck and one front and back on my upper left arm. I hoped three was the charm, and I'd make it to old age with only those as badges of honor.

But I doubted it.

The remnants of cholla spines in my leg festered from time to time and I scraped pustules away every other day. I was a bit of a wreck but I wasn't going to let it slow me down.

Cade Tolliver, Mexican Bob, Carlos Apaza, and Shorty McFearson were still breathing free clean air, and I meant to change that.

The gray had enjoyed a good rest and being grained twice so we made the thirty miles at a quick walk alternating with a ground-eating lope. It was well past sundown when I reined up to study the Skunk Valley Trading Post. No lights shone in the post window, but the house shone oil lamps and a whisper of smoke from the chimney.

No animals were tied to the hitching rails.

Still, caution ruled, so I tied the gray back in the trees and did a quiet walk up to the house, stood quiet just listening but hearing nothing untoward, knocked quietly.

Gustav answered. He carried a shotgun in one hand and pushed me off the porch with the other.

He had a knot on his head the size of half a hen's egg and his eye was badly blackened.

"You have ruined our lives," he spat, aiming the shotgun at me as I stood with hands out, palms facing him showing no threat. "Anna will never forgive you and I should shoot you down like the dog you are."

Seems I'd fallen out of favor with the Johansons.

Chapter Twenty

I was about to break and run when Anna screamed at Gustav. "It wasn't Conn, you old fool!"

He yelled back, "Wouldn't a' happened had he not stirred up them good for nothin's."

"Put the shotgun down, Gustav," I said, with some authority in my voice.

Anna yelled again, "You hurt that boy you'll be washing your own long John's and making your own vittles!"

He slowly lowered the scatter gun as I asked, "What happened?"

Anna walked up beside him. "Tolliver, Bob, and three others charged in here, took what they wanted..." and she began to cry, "and...and took Elena."

That sat me back on my heels. "Took her? Took her against her will?"

Anna sobbed while Gustav explained, "Mexican Bob knocked me cold then Anna said dragged Elena out, kicking and screamin' until Bob slapped her silly. They took a horse and two mules and pack gear from our barn, which was fine as it was some Hector led in from their camp...but which they loaded up with our goods without paying so much as a thin dime. Bob bound Elena's wrists to the horn and dragged her off behind him."

The heat flooded my backbone until I thought I'd scream, but rather I calmed myself and asked, "Off where?"

Gustav answered, "They rode out south toward Wickenburg. I come around right away and followed for a couple of miles until they took a pot shot at me. For a while I was too dang dizzy to ride. I'm riding on into town to alert the marshal then to the telegraph to alert the whole damn territory."

"How long ago?" I asked.

"Rode in here at noon, rode out about one o'clock.'"

"You say three others besides Tolliver and Bob?"

"One of 'em they picked up at their camp. Seems they had a cave in what I overheard and two was buried and one, heard Tolliver call him Lucas, crawled out and lived. He rode in on a tall bay but traded for that big half draft Hector had brung. So it was Tolliver, Mexican Bob, Dutch who some call Lucas, Apaza, and Shorty."

I nodded, searching my memory. "Saw his name on a poster in Sheriff Beaumont's office. Lucas Van Horn, big blond galoot, right?"

Anna answered. "That's him. One of the others called him Dutch also."

Nodding, I was feeling pretty smart as I'd nicknamed him Dutch as well. I thought for a moment, then ordered, not asked, "I'm gonna stock up a little. Gustav, you load the roan up with my packsaddle and paniers and my Sharps. I'll get on their trail and stop at Wickenburg long enough to alert the sheriff and law territory wide. You stay with Anna. She needs a man at her side."

He actually looked relieved and nodded his head as Anna reassured him. "You're too dang long in the tooth to be riding for days...'sides, with your eyesight you couldn't hit the barn out back much less some brigands."

"Hell I couldn't," he said, a little adamant,

then relented, "then again, you do need a man about."

"Thank you," she said, relieved he'd come to his senses, and he seemed relieved she'd given him an out. Then she added, "While you're fixin' to go I'll put together some grub to fill those paniers."

I'd learned a lot from my Yavapai friend Hooch, and some of that was the fine points of tracking. We'd talked game, not men, but horses were much the same as tracking antelope, deer, or elk, so I headed out front and studied the tracks of the most recent horses to pass by or tie up. One of the sets of tracks stood out. It was a bigger animal, shoes near half again the size of most horses. Not big enough to be a draft animal, but maybe a cross. Another of the animals wore a shoe with a notch that was clear as a beautiful Sunday morning. I couldn't have marked it better myself had I taken a file to it. The rest could be any horse near any time and place. I walked on out to the barn where Gustav was doing my bidding.

"Anything you can tell me about their mounts?" I asked.

"Tolliver was on that handsome chestnut. He always tied him away from others so maybe a stud. Lucas was on what looked to be half Clydesdale or Percheron. A dun with white sox and a blaze. Lucas must weigh well over two fifty, maybe near three hundred pounds. Others atop a black, a light gray near white, and a pinto...maybe a piebald or skewbald. The mules...by the way one of them wasn't shod...are both blacks. The horse Bob took for Elena was a sort of faded out palomino, mare with lots of white in her, with white sox and blaze."

I repeated it back to him, making sure I put it to memory.

Anna joined us in the barn with two sacks, almost more than she could carry, and Gustav and I hoisted them into the roan's paniers, then I threw a tarp and diamond hitch over the load and mounted up.

"Go with God," Anna said.

And Gustav, to his credit, added, "In your debt, young Conn. Use that Sharps from two hundred yards and you'll stay out of range of them worthless dogs. You bring Elena back to us."

"Yes, sir," I said, and doffed my hat to Anna. "You try and not worry too much. I'll put the five of them in the ground and keep Elena safe."

And I was off at a lope, dragging the roan behind. Luckily the roan didn't take to being dragged and moved up alongside where the trail allowed and the road to Wickenburg was a two-track so easy traveling, even in the dark. My left shoulder pained me so leading the roan with the left was out of the question.

After a couple of hours I slowed to a walk. The waning moon gave little light and if the gang reined off the road I didn't want to miss it. Finally it got too dark to see much and a row of cotton-woods crossed the trail, and as I hoped was centered with a trickle of water so I swung off, watered and picket pinned the horses, dropped their tack, and unrolled and slept until a hard rain awakened me. I used the canvas bedroll for a makeshift tent, leaning against a fat cottonwood until the rain clouds moved away. The rain was a curse but also a blessing. Rain might obliterate their tracks until it stopped but then fresh mud would make new tracks much easier to follow. Just as a fine line of orange showed in the east I packed up and we lit out.

The big horse and heavy rider, Dutch, made deep tracks and even the rain hadn't washed them away, so I was able to move at a comfortable lope. As we neared Wickenburg, maybe a mile out, I lost the trail so doubled back and found where they'd veered off to the east. I guess avoiding the town. The road from Wickenburg to Maricopa

Wells would be easily found, and I had to conclude they were headed south even if they didn't head into town. Besides, I'm sure many with the stage lines would recognize the gang members and why risk it. They'd provisioned up at the Johanson's. So, I headed in to keep my word, advise the city marshal and the rest of the territory by sending telegrams to Yuma, Maricopa Wells, Prescott, and the forts, Apache, Whipple, Bowie, and Verde. All of that conditioned upon the fact the wire had arrived at those locals. I'd likely keep it to those as a fella could rapidly go broke sending telegrams at over a dime a word.

At the marshal's suggestion I left him two dollars as a young man he knew was a fine artist and would ride out to the Johanson's and with their help draw a likeness of Elena for a flyer, which he promised to have printed and to distribute to the express companies to haul where they might do some good. In less than an hour I headed on south out of Wickenburg. It was my hope I'd cut their trail somewhere on the road to the Vulture Mine before it turned southeast to Maricopa Wells and that they hadn't merely gone around Wickenburg and would continue due south through the Growler Mountains on their way to Sonora and old Mexico.

I had few words in Spanish, so if the gang led me across the border and deep into Sonora, I'd likely have to hire an interpreter. I could find my way to the *banos*, to a *resterante*, a *medico, juscado, or cantina*, but that was about it.

Sure as there's a good Lord to help us along I cut their trail re-joining the road not a mile south of town—deep track of the half draft and heavy man, notched track of another—and again gigged the gray into a lope. I know it's just a smidgen more than a hundred twenty miles from Wickenburg to Maricopa Wells on the banks of the Gila River, but I'd long ago decided I'd ride to the hubs of hell to avenge Sarah Ann, and now to rescue Elena.

Chapter Twenty-One

I was getting so hungry my gut was growling like a Sonora wolf after a fat jack rabbit, but stopping was out of the question... unless I spotted the right critters among those lining the street or being boarded at the hostler.

Riding straight on through the mining town of Vulture City I paid little attention to anything other than the stock tied up to hitching rails. I saw none of the most identifiable, the chestnut, pinto or half draft. It was no wild boomtown as there was little outside a tiny church, the company store, the saloon—with a sign saying only open from six p.m. Saturday night to midnight, then from one o'clock after church to nine p.m.—some cabins I'd guess for married employees, and a few buildings which appeared be bunkhouses for the unmarried. There was a hostelry, but with only a tiny office building, a shed for a blacksmith and a shed to keep rain off the hay and bins of oats and grain. The only building of any distinction was the express company, it with a generous corral and twenty horse barn. As Wickenburg was twelve miles from Vulture City, the stage station was there. I knew there would be another some fifteen miles on toward Maricopa and another every fifteen miles or so...unless a water hole dictated more or less.

The road soon was easing southeast. After a few miles of alternating lope and walk, I had reason to suddenly rein up and again study the track.

Sweeping in from the southwest came another set of tracks. These too many to determine, and worse occluding the gang's tracks. But far worse, these all-unshod animals. I can only conclude a band of renegade Apaches.

This threw a whole new light on riding down the Tolliver gang. If a couple of dozen wild Apache were between the gang and me, I'd have to rethink how I was going to extract my revenge and rescue Elena. The Apache might exact my revenge for me, not that I'd favor that solution as it was my hope to watch those who'd been in on her death fall by my sword. And to complicate things more, if the Indians did overrun and slay the Tolliver gang, they'd likely spare the beautiful Elena death as they'd have their own use of her. Rescuing her from a band of five was a whole different matter than from a band of twenty-five, maybe more.

General Crook and his troop had ridden down most the Apache but those not in reservations were the worst of them. If they'd escaped his army, they knew the country, could live a week on a chuckwalla lizard, and could lay in wait in a scorching desert sun while your horse and you passed within a half dozen paces without a glance until they were on your back sawing at your topknot.

I had a few words of Yavapai, thanks to Hooch, but could only hope the Apache might understand, and could hope even more I wouldn't have the opportunity to try my linguistic skills.

The devil of it was, there was nothing to do but charge on.

It was well after dark when I spotted a window and light likely from a coal oil lantern, then reined up in front of what the sign said was Whippoorwill Stage Station. I had just dismounted and could hear in the distance the pounding of hooves and rattle of trace chains. Then, nearby, around the corner of the adobe building came the station master leading a harnessed six-up.

"Howdy," he yelled at me. "Didn't hear you and the damn dog didn't bark. He's gonna get me kilt."

"Howdy, how's chances for a little grub?"

"You're just in time. Ma's feeding the passengers and if you got four bits, you can join right in. Antelope stew, apple pie, biscuits—"

"For that I got four bits."

"Mind tying your critters around to the side. Wagon is rolling in..."

"You bet," I said and untied and led my gray and roan to the side of the station. Then yelled back at him, "Can I help?"

"Son, I can do this in my sleep. In fact think I have a time or two. Go on inside and beat these passengers to the coffee and grub."

The loaded wagon rolled in with some well-lathered mules and the station master went to work. Taking his advice, I was seated with a bowl of stew and biscuit as eight passengers, the whip, and the guard piled in a took a seat at the long table. Two women were among them, dressed to travel in soft skirts and blouses, sunburned even with bonnets. I'd taken the head of the table, so had a clear view of the bunch. The whip, who looked as if he was born in the seat and had spent all of near sixty years there, a short fella but with shoulders an axe handle wide, sat at my right and extended a calloused hand. "Sirus Beaureguard," he offered, and I shook and returned the favor, "Conn Donahey." The shotgun guard, tall, lanky, a hawk nose and piercing eyes near gold colored, seated himself to my left. He did not introduce himself.

Beaureguard eyed me carefully, then asked, "You the fella kilt some road agents a few days ago?"

As Doc Holliday had warned me about reputation, I was a little slow to answer, then finally fessed up. "Times is a fella has to pull a trigger, like it or not."

The guard drilled me with those eyes, and wasn't bashful about who heard, "Some son of a bitch back shot 'em from the weeds is the way I heard it."

Right or wrong it made me suddenly hot under the collar. "Were you there, maybe with a mask on?"

That brought him to his feet so quickly he knocked the chair over behind, so I stood to face him only an arm's length away. He growled, "By God, you're reckless with your mouth." His hand rested on the bone grips of the revolver at his side.

"Set the hell down, Petersen...you asked for it," Beaureguard yelled at him.

The guard looked from the whip to me and back again to him. The whip motioned, pointing down, and the guard uprighted his chair and sat just as the lady of the station arrived with a big bowl and ladle. Before she served him stew, she chastised him.

"Orval, you want to put your skinny ass at my table, you'll mind your manners."

"This whelp accused me of being a road agent."

"He answered your insult and I'm surprised he didn't turn that bowl over your ugly head. Now, if you can't be cordial, take yourself outside."

The guard, who I took to be Orval Petersen, nodded and sat quiet and she served him. He mumbled, "Sorry, Miss Martha. We'll finish this discussion after dinner...outside."

"Fine by me," I said and eyed the others at the table. Two of the men looked to be drummers or at least city fellas traveling, two others who had each escorted the ladies to the table had on rough clothes and were likely farmers or stockmen, and the last two had on the dress of the range other than fancy waistcoats and tooled, tied down holsters and second revolvers, maybe smaller sheriff's model Colt's, one with a rig under his left shoulder, the other with a butt-forward rig on his left hip. Both of them wore wide sombreros which they, impolitely, left on at the table. The strangest item of their attire was red sashes worn tied around their waist. I wondered if they might be vaqueros or gauchos up from Argentina or some such, but they spoke in low tones in English.

Both were unshaven, both had an arrogance about them that put me on guard.

Chapter Twenty-Two

I decided discretion the better part of valor and ignored them as the mistress of the station served them. I did give the ladies a nod, before I returned to my seat. "Ladies," I said, apologizing for the guard, "you'll pardon the language," then turned to Sirus. "I came across the track of a couple of dozen unshod horses on up the road aways. You see any Indians?"

"Nary a one."

"How about some fellas riding with a young woman, one of them on a handsome chestnut? Another big fella on a half-draft. Hard to miss."

"Half a day back some half dozen horse backers reined fifty paces off the road well ahead of us and sat in the poor shade of some mesquite and watched us pass. I found it a bit odd. Put it off to them not wantin' to eat our dust...but could be they didn't want us to eyeball 'em close up."

I nodded, happy to hear I was likely close on their trail. Then he asked, "You the law?"

"Nope." I started to add, "they'll wish I was," but kept it to myself.

The station master, I guess finished with switching the team, came in and walked past to the kitchen, doffing his hat to the ladies and asking as he passed, "How's the stew?" But not waiting for an answer he disappeared through the door.

"Passable," one of the women said to the closed door, and both she and the other laughed.

I thought it fine and all those at the table, including the women were digging in.

The guard gave me several hard looks as I ate, but I ignored him as I finished an exceptional piece of apple pie. As I'd started before the others, and was eager to get on the road, I rose first with a "Please pardon me, ladies."

But the guard wouldn't let it rest. "You running off, piker?"

I ignored him, dropped four bits on the table, and headed for the door.

He stood and again knocked the chair over and came close behind me.

As it looked like he meant to do me harm I exited but only took four strides outside into a now dark night, then turned back.

"Hold up, backshooter," he yelled as he charged out, leaving the door open as he came.

I put my weight and my years of blacksmithing into the right and although I aimed for the beak that was his nose, caught him on the chin. I was not surprised as, with arms windmilling, he flew back inside and landed flat on his back and lay there with nary a twitch. The whip, Sirus, had to step aside as he was following.

Sirus stood looking down at him, then glanced over to me. "Hope you didn't kill him? I need him all the way to Wickenburg."

I gave him a nod. "Hope I knocked some sense into him."

"Sense he could use, but don't be holding your breath," Sirus said.

Then the two with the red sashes came striding out as if they had a purpose, stepping over the guard.

I stayed a half dozen strides ahead of them moving on around the side of the adobe where my stock was tied. I was not comfortable with them following and stepped behind the gray, slipping the coach gun from its scabbard.

One of the two, the ugliest one, yelled at me as they stomped my way. "That was a friend of our'n."

They both lay hands on the butts of their revolvers, so I cocked both barrels of the scattergun—amazing how loud is the cocking of deadly weapon—and stepped out into the clear, not exactly aiming at them, but near enough they knew I was a tenth of a second from letting fly.

I cautioned them. "Could be it's too dark for you two to see you're looking down these barrels at eighteen fat lead buckshot." They stopped short, and hands drifted away from revolvers as I said, with steadiness and a slow serious pace. "Y'all should be more careful about who you friend up with."

The ugly one gave me a hard stare. "I hear'd you say you was Donahey?"

"You hear'd right," I said, mocking him a little.

"We done hear'd about you, and won't forget you."

"Memories fade away when your soul takes flight. Suggest you go back to that pie. You won't find a better apple pie anywhere in the territory."

They looked at each other then back at me, then backed away, turned, and rounded the corner.

I mounted up and rode around the back of the adobe rather than give them the cover of a doorway which I'd hesitate to fire into as beyond it was full of innocents. I waited until I had forty yards down the wagon road into the dark of night, then let the hammers down and re-booted the coach gun when they had not appeared out the door and gigged the gray and roan into a lope.

When I slowed the critters to a brisk walk, I couldn't help but wonder if it wouldn't be wise to change my name. I had cousins, who I hadn't seen in more than a dozen years, the Callihans.

Dang if Conn Callihan didn't sound like a fine handle.

I only rode for a couple of miles then reined off where I saw a flat open spot among the mesquite where there seemed to be quite a bit of grass and made a dry camp. The big bowl of stew, biscuit and pie made me sleepy. As I needed no fire and I was over fifty paces from the road, no one would bother us in the night.

The wind woke me just as the sky was coloring and we were on the road before the sun lined the mountains in the far distance to our left.

The road led out a little east of south and I knew from talk Petersburg and the crossing of the Gila River was only occupied by a stage station and a half dozen farmers who'd been able to build a mile-and-a-half-long irrigation ditch. It was said the river was wide and only six inches deep, so the teams barely had to slow.

As we moved along, I loaded up on some jerky and hardtack Miss Anna had stuffed in my saddlebags. I really wanted to slice up and fry some of the side pork there but sure I could gain on the Tolliver bunch, so I kept up a brisk walk while I gnawed, then took up the lope.

Again, I was alternating between a brisk walk and a lope, so making good time.

Even at the pace we were keeping I kept a close eye out for Indians. I'd made no more unshod track, but that didn't mean they were not near the road somewhere awaiting easy pickings. I was particularly careful as we moved through some very large saguaro. Judging it to be four p.m. as my stomach was again flapping against my backbone and I knew the horses were needing water, I kept my eyes peeled for signs of a wet spot, maybe cottonwoods. And Indians. A man could easily hide, standing with bow or rifle in hand behind a forty-foot tall, three-foot-thick saguaro.

Luckily, I saw nothing to get my heartbeat up. Then I topped a rise and my heartbeat raced. I didn't see, but heard.

Gunfire, and it wasn't a hunter as it was rapid and frequent.

Chapter Twenty-Three

I'm pretty sure my mentor, Doc, would say it was only a damn fool who'd ride into gunfire, but my task called me on.

The mesquite was thick and the sun off to my left, thank God not in my eyes. I moved over a half mile as gunfire waxed and waned. Whatever the battle was all about it had several on each side. The gunfire, as I neared, assured me I needed to know who was fighting who and if I got any nearer I was likely to discover who as I got an ounce of lead between the shoulders. I could see the tops of a few narrow-leaf cottonwoods above the mesquite in the distance, so maybe a spring, and a spring maybe the next stage station...the distance seemed about right.

Spotting a rise topped with an outcropping of

rock on the far side of the road away from the cottonwoods, I reined off the road and closed the fifty yards to it, then picketed the horses near. With the 73 in one hand, I pulled the Sharps from its boot on the packsaddle on the roan, and climbed the rockpile.

It was a stage station, obvious by the Concord pulled up on the far side of the adobe building so I could only see the back half. The station was at least one hundred yards north of the now north-west by southeast road. Wagon, but no teams. It was strange that neither the incoming or outgoing team was in sight, the wagon sat, luggage in the boot and a couple of pieces on top. The front door of the station was maybe one hundred fifty or sixty yards from my perch, with the road between us. With the rifle reports, puffs of gun smoke came from gun ports, holes in the heavy plank shutters covering the adobe station windows. From the ends of rafter logs sticking through the walls I could see the walls rose above the roof. It was flat-roofed and I quickly made out firing portals like pictures of English castles I'd seen. Portals where the occasional barrel showed, where muzzle flashes and smoke bellowed from them.

Just as I settled in, I saw a couple of Apache

move to relocate their firing position. It was clear to me that if I was to take sides, even if the Cade Tolliver gang was in the adobe, my side in this battle had to be on that of the white man.

In this case, the white men who likely had Elena among them.

I could only see the two Apache who I'd seen relocate. The saguaro were more sparse here, only a few among the mesquite. I'd had to dodge some cholla while making my way to the rocks, but they were sparse as well.

Traveling along, when I'd found myself in a lonely camp and it was still light I'd reloaded some of the dozen brass cartridges that had come with the handheld reloading press and priming tool. There was also a bullet mold and a pound of lead, but a dozen formed bullets were among the folderol. Six finished cartridges were with the rifle and I'd finished eight more. I'd picked a rock two hundred yards distant and kicked up dirt just below and again just above, so was confident with its accuracy. My shoulder decided it was a hell of a rifle. Now I only hoped I'd done the loads correctly for all of them. I had twelve loaded and primed cartridges left, should all of them be sound. With that concern, I started with the six, trusting whoever had loaded them more than myself.

I sighted in the nearest Indian, who was firing from a position behind a saguaro, then realized he was only a little over a hundred yards and I had boxes of .44-40 so switched to the 73. The rocks made a great rest, so I lay down on him and guess I hit him in the butt or a thigh as he stumbled away, dragging a leg, until out of sight. I could likely have hit him again but my pa, returning from the war, said at times a wounded man was of more use to his enemy than a dead one, as the wounded man had to be cared for and that consumed men and resources. The second Indian was maybe ten yards farther and I'm sure presumed his fellow brave had been hit from firing from the adobe as his attention remained that way.

I adjusted my point of target up and this time, the rifle bucked in my hands and the second brave grabbed for the saguaro to keep his feet but it didn't help. He dropped his rifle and only stumbled three paces before he sagged on his face in a cholla, unmoving. Changing positions, I moved ten feet to my right, found another good spot but could see no more savages...but they were about as firing continued from the chaparral and the adobe.

Between the house and barn was all corral, maybe ten feet wider than the house on both sides. Several head of stock milled about in the corral as gunfire rattled the air all around. Centered in that corral was one of the new-fangled windmills at least twenty-five feet high to catch the breeze, with a trough below. There was also a corral behind the barn. The house was abode but the barn forty or so paces behind was mesquite, the crooked dry branches had been bound together and the roof was the same but covered with what appeared to be cottonwood bark in layers.

I saw an Indian appear out of the brush behind the barn, cross the small corral with a flaming torch in hand, but before I could lay sights on him, he disappeared behind the barn. I could see the torch arch up and land on the roof, but I paid closer attention where the Indian had emerged from the heavy stand of mesquite. This had to be near two hundred yards, so I recovered the Sharps, and quickly adjusted the Pedersoli long-range sights for two hundred yards.

He did not disappoint, but as soon as the roof flamed up, appeared. I tracked him across the little corral and when he bent and paused to duck between the rails, pulled off. The .45-90 is not a .44-40 and the recoil damn near knocked me into the rocks behind my stance.

And it was no surprise it knocked the brave through the rails and he hit on the far side, unmoving.

What I'd failed to consider was the roar of that .45-90 was unlike anything the Indians had, which suddenly made it clear to them that they had an enemy somewhere in the mesquite, saguaro, and rocks.

A slug kicked rock shards in my face and sang a death song as it ricocheted off the stone and spun away behind me, then another was so close it tickled my ear. I ducked, gathered up my Sharps and 73 and maneuvered between the rocks back to the horses, slipped their picket pins, mounted the gray, stayed low on his withers, and gave him heels heading to the adobe while leading the roan.

I knew exactly where I was heading and into what as among the stock in the corral around the windmill trough was a beautiful sixteen-hand chestnut.

But it seemed I had little choice.

Chapter Twenty-Four

Just as I'd mounted, still carrying the reloaded Sharps, an arrow slammed into the loaded saddlebag on the left side and another whizzed under my right arm to disappear in the rock pile. Luckily, I'd gigged the gray with hard heels and he leaped as a bullet buzzed, hornet-like, by my ear. We rounded the rocks and an Indian, so dusky in color and covered with skins he nearly disappeared against the desert floor, was directly in front, between us and the cabin, and luckily facing the adobe. The gray shied from him. But I whacked him a good one across the back of his head with the heavy barrel of the Sharps as we passed.

He flopped face first next to the thick saguaro.

Then I crouched low against the gray's withers as we pounded for the cabin. They must have seen me coming as the door flew open as I neared. I wasn't about to leave my critters, guns, loaded saddlebags and paniers outside for the Apache, so ducked nearly to level with the gray's back as I reined the animals thru the door. It seemed a bit of a surprise to those inside. However they seemed to appreciate the reinforcements as I slid from the saddle, slipping the 73 from its boot, and yelled at a gray-haired lady as I passed, "Drop the saddles and put 'em out the back door in the corral."

She yelled back. "Barn's on fire, they may all leap the rails and them dirty Apache will have 'em."

"Then leave my two inside. Women and children might need to pound trail if it comes to that. That scattergun is loaded should they try and come through the door."

"Obliged," she managed as I scampered for a ladder to climb to the roof.

Th ladder led to a trapdoor in the ceiling. And I scrambled up, a little clumsy with a long arm in each hand.

Cade Tolliver, Dutch, and another fella unknown to me, were at gun portals, each facing a different direction. As far as I knew none of them had ever laid eyes on me so I had no reason to expect a slug between my shoulders as I took up a position at the only wall not occupied.

I had not searched every nook and corner of the adobe as I'd quickly moved through. And it was two rooms and I couldn't see into what I presumed was a bedroom, so had no idea where the other two gang members and Elena might be. I'd already decided the instant I laid eyes on Mexican Bob, he was a dead man even if it meant one less gun against the Indians. So far I didn't have time to worry about it as a volley of gunfire knocked chunks out of the rampart wall rising above the nearly flat roof and other lead buzzed overhead.

Tolliver yelled at me, "Welcome stranger. Seems you rode into it."

I was busy searching the chaparral for a target but yelled back over my shoulder, "Dang if I didn't, but didn't have nothing else to do."

He chuckled, then turned his attention back to his firing portal, snapped his rifle to his thick shoulder and fired.

I fired nary a shot as I spotted no savages.

The silence became deafening. No sound, other than the crackling and falling mesquite logs from the burning barn and the neighing of the horses in the corral who were now packed up against the adobe.

Finally, the big gang member, Dutch, spoke up. "I do believe them dirty Apache have taken flight."

"Agreed," Tolliver said, although he was still surveying the mesquite thicket.

The fella unknown to me left his post and walked over and extended his hand. He was bald, bearded, and salt and pepper gray. "Tobias McGruder, station master," he offered.

"Conn Callihan," I answered and shook. I sure as hell wasn't going to use my real name in front of Tolliver and Dutch.

"We thank you for joining up with us," Tobias said.

Tolliver walked over and extended his hand, with Dutch close behind. "Cade, and that's Dutch," he said, not offering his last name which I already knew.

I shook, then turned to Tobias. "Who's down below?"

"Two passengers and the driver and shotgun messenger. And my wife and son and daughter, Thomas and Tilly...Matilda." Then to turned to Tolliver. "We might as well go down."

Tolliver turned to Dutch. "You stay up and keep watch. Let's make sure they ain't just off figuring how to breech the walls."

Tobias shook his head. "Bastards got both teams, twelve horses. Drove them off almost before we knew they was on us. Lucky I was next to the coach and jumped in and they didn't bother with me. I figure they were happy with the haul. But others of them fired on the house."

"Both teams?" I asked.

"I was changing teams when they hit us. Drove off both teams, still in harness. When I'm sure they've hightailed it I'll track them and odds are find the rigs as them savages got no use for it."

"Don't count on it, lots of use for leather and trace chains. You got another team?" I asked.

"I can rig another four-up, but not until I recover the harness or go into harness makin'. They'll be piss poor pullers as none of the stock left'll make a decent wheel or lead horse. Let's go out and knock the fire down on what's left of the barn. We'll have to rig a fence on that end."

We descended the ladder and when down I passed among those gathered there and introduced myself. The passengers were a couple, Kirby-Jones their last name. The driver was a skinny runt who called himself "Cajun Jesse" and the shotgun messenger or guard gave me a nod and announced, "Moonshine Williams, most call me just Moony." Mexican Bob and Elena were not among them. The third member of the gang, Carlos Apaza, walked out from the backroom and gave me a nod and, "Just call me Jose. Jose will do just fine, amigo." He was hard to miss and I knew he was lying as I'd seen a poster on him in Sheriff Beaumont's office. The pearl eye confirmed his identity.

Tobias introduced his missus, a woman of generous girth who wore an old-fashioned dust cap over stringy dirty-blond hair, seemed to be twenty years younger than her husband but sturdy and up to the job of station mistress. And their children, Tilly and Thomas. Tilly maybe fifteen and Thomas a couple of years younger. Tobias, looking at least sixty, had started his family late.

So, Mexican Bob, Elena, and Billy Bob Ten Gauge were missing.

As we exited the adobe, Tobias commanded his wife, "Missus, you and Tilly get some fixin's on the table. Time we done et"—then turned to his son—"Thomas, you get up the ladder and give that fella another pair of eyes. Wouldn't do to be snuck up on."

"Yes, Pa," the boy said, and ran for the ladder.

All the men, other than Apaza, moved out into the corral, through the ten head of stock there, six horses and four mules, and started using the three available buckets to form a line from the trough below the windmill. Lined up, we started dousing what was left of the barn. A stack of loose hay was badly burned and two bins of grain were burned down to the fill line, the contents badly burned and scorched.

While I passed full buckets one way and empty the other, I was planning how to go about either putting the remaining members of the Tolliver gang in the ground, or bound up for a trip to Maricopa Wells and the law...although I'd much prefer the former.

Chapter Twenty-Five

Prefer or not, I couldn't bring myself to shove my Colt in the small of Cade's back and pull the trigger. Then again, it would be hell, one man trying to get three back to a jail that could hold them. My tack was still piled in a corner so as Tolliver mounted the ladder to call Dutch to eat, I casually slipped the coach gun from its scabbard and leaned it against the wall. I would get my chance.

Then Apaza confirmed my decision.

On returning inside, the fire now a smoking charred hulk of the former barn, Tobias looked around then turned to his wife. "Where's Tilly?"

"I sent her to the tater cellar for some onions. Where is that girl?"

And Mrs. Kirby-Jones chimed in, "That fella, the one with the bad eye, followed her out."

I turned to Tobias, "I saw a cellar door out near the hitching rail—"

Before I could answer, Tobias was striding toward the front door.

Tolliver was back with his feet flat on the well-packed dirt floor and palmed his Colt before Tobias reached for the latch. He was half turned away from my stance near the door out to the back.

"Hey, Pilgrim, you hold up," Tolliver said, and Tobias turned to be looking down the barrel of Tolliver's revolver. Mrs. Kirby-Jones was an attractive young woman as well, and I could see the worst was about to happen. Tolliver continued as Tobias looked from Tolliver to the door, then we heard the muffled scream of his daughter below the floorboards.

"By God..." Tobias said and reached for the latch.

Tolliver cocked the revolver, but he was a half second too late.

I'd cocked both barrels of the coach gun as I swung it up and pulled one off on him as soon as it leveled. The load took him half on his upper left arm and half in his chest about heart high. He spun a complete circle and went down in a heap, I started to move to make sure he was out of it then realized the big Dutchman was descending the ladder, gun in hand. Before he could see what was going on below, I blew his legs out from under him with the second barrel.

He hit the floor rattling the whole house, and, to Mr. Kirby-Jones credit he took two strides and kicked the weapon out of the Dutchman's hand. It went flying. I guess I'd hit that big vein in his leg as he was pumping blood as he lay on his back gasping for air probably having the wind knocked out of him with the fall. He was gushing blood with heart-pump regularity faster than the windmill outside was refilling the trough. He wouldn't last long.

Tobias ran for the outside and the root cellar. I yelled at him. "That man's armed."

But he paid no attention. I needed information so I quickly moved over, revolver in hand, and leaned down over the Dutchman. "Where's Elena?"

"Bugger you," he managed.

"I can stop that bleeding with a tourniquet, but not until you tell me where Elena is?"

"Night before last...Mexican Bob cut Ten Gauge's gizzard out as he had his hands on her, then Bob and the girl snuck out in the night. Guess he wasn't gonna...gonna share...gonna share the...the little chile pepper."

"Where's Ten Gauge's body?"

A few hundred...few hundred yards...back up the trail. Left him leaning against a single big ol'...big old dead cottonwood."

"Where's Mexican Bob headed?"

"He's got...got family...down in Mexico. You gonna—"

But he was fading fast and didn't finish the question.

About that time, I heard another gunshot and ran for the outside. I got there just in time to see the root cellar door open and Tobias, gun in one hand, stumbling back holding his side with the other and blood gushing between his fingers. I sidestepped up beside the stairway leading down under the house, but not where I'd make a target.

"Apaza, throw your weapons out and come on out of there."

Tobias's wife, screaming, ran out the door to her husband, now down on one knee. As Apaza could likely see her, I kicked the door shut.

The Kirby-Jones couple was right behind the mistress of the station and I yelled to them, "Get him inside and pressure on that wound."

Mrs. Magruder spun as the couple helped him inside. "Where's Tilly. Get Tilly."

"She's still down in the root cellar. I'm talking him...and Tilly...out of there. You tend your husband."

She eyed me, eyed the root cellar door, then back at me. So, I insisted, "I'll get her out of there. Your husband needs you."

I was happy she ran inside as I didn't want to have to worry about the girl, her, and myself.

Yelling again at Apaza, I got nearer the door. "You aren't going anywhere, Carlos Apaza. Tolliver and the Dutchman are both dead."

He yelled back. "Maybe, but I got the girl."

"You got yourself in a hole like a rat. Whatever you think you can do to the girl, it's gonna be done tenfold to you." Then I lied, "This place and these people don't make a tinker's damn to me. I'll burn this place down with you and the girl to cook."

He's silent for a moment, then yells back. "Adobe don't burn...and how'd you know our names?"

"Don't matter. Tell you what. Which horse is yours?"

"The pinto...saddle black with a vaquero horn."

"I'll have him saddled and waiting right by the door. When I give you a yell, you leave the girl and you can ride off."

Again, there's a long silence. "There's a set of neck bags on Tolliver's saddle. You move them to my pinto and you got a deal."

And again, I lied like a politician running for office. "Sure, all I want is to get after my lady friend Elena. Keep your hands off Tilly while I get the pinto and bags."

"I ain't touchin' the *gringa*, unless I got to gut her like a catfish should you lie to me."

"As ye sow...give me five minutes," I said but stuck my head in the door and spoke to Thomas and Kirby-Jones, low enough I hoped Apaza couldn't hear. "Saddle the pinto. Grab the neck saddlebags and dump the contents on the table there then rig them on the pinto, and lead him around here." They ran out the back way. I crossed the room to my gear and grabbed the Sharps and returned and leaned it just inside the doorway, then moved back to the cellar door.

I yelled, "Saddling up and switching the bags over now. You gonna keep your word, Apaza?"

"As God is my witness, gringo. Question is, are you?"

"All I want is that little girl set free, you on your way, and me after my lady Elena. *Comprendo?*"

"Then *vamos*."

It was silence for a moment, then I heard what I was sure was gold coins and bars being dumped onto the table. Again I stuck my head in the doorway and with little more than a whisper instructed, "Fill them with something, anything."

Thomas grabbed the potatoes and carrots his mother had half peeled for supper and stuffed them in the bags, then topped one side off with a tablecloth and the other with cloth dishrags.

He ran back and in moments appeared around the side of the station leading the pinto, saddled and bridled, the neck bags in place.

"Get back inside," I instructed the boy, and he ran inside and pulled the door shut behind.

"Pinto is here and ready to go," I yelled to Apaza.

Chapter Twenty-Six

"You back off," Apaza yelled at me, "all the way around the side of the house."

"I'll back off, but you let the girl go free first."

"You're a funny *gringo, gringo*. We're coming out. The girl will walk with me, close behind me, close enough I can feel her breath on the back of my neck, a hundred paces and if I see no one at a hundred paces, I will mount up and ride away like the wind."

"I will yell when I'm around the corner."

I moved that way, but on the way stuck my head in the door, grabbed the Sharps, and yelled at those inside loud enough for Apaza to hear. "Y'all stay inside SeñorApaza is riding away, but not mounting up and turning Tilly loose until he's a hundred paces away. And not then if he sees anyone, anyone, in sight."

I backed off and around the corner of the station. Only then did I yell. "Out of sight, Apaza."

It was all I could do not to step out with my Colt in hand, but it would mean risking Tilly and I couldn't do that. I waited, counting off a hundred about as fast as a man would walk, then peeked around the corner. True to his word he was moving away, seeming with the girl behind him but her hands around his waist and him locking her hands together in front of him. He took three or four more paces, turned and shoved her away, and with the horse breaking into a run, swung into the saddle. I was happy he'd shoved her as she was out of the path of the .45-90.

He was nearing one hundred fifty yards at a full gallop, Tilly running full tilt back our way but off to the side of the two-track. The damn fool, Apaza, was staying in the road when he could have easily broke off into the mesquite and out of sight.

The Pedersoli sights were set for two hundred yards so I was in no hurry. Besides, he was going up a slight rise and the farther he got the less risk to Tilly. With the corner of the building as a rest I lined up, took my time, and squeezed.

Even with the heavy barrel the Sharps bucked in my hands. There was no doubt the true of my aim as his hands flew up and he did a forward flip over the right wither of the pinto.

I quickly opened the breech, ejected the shell and seated another. But there was no need.

Eight down, one more to go.

I don't believe I've ever seen a woman run so fast as Tilly did, holding her skits high with both hands. Walking that way, I had to stop and watch her pass. She didn't say a word or give me even a glance, but flew by like a wolf was nipping at her heels and was in her mother's arms before I continued my stroll. Made me feel kinda good to see them both bawling and hugging.

The pinto was either well trained or just naturally curious. He'd run another twenty-five yards and stopped and turned, then clomped back and we arrived at Apaza who wasn't in as big a pool of blood as I expected. The shot took him dead center heart high and I guess his pumper quit on him before he hit the ground. I didn't feel a moment of remorse.

He had a Remington Frontier Single Action Army in one holster, a fine stag handled knife in a hair-out sheath on his belt, and a belly gun in a sewn pocket on the outer thigh opposite the Remington. I gathered up all three and started my trek back. Then stopped. The handsome black sombrero he'd worn had rolled off the side. I strode back and tried it on and dang if it didn't fit perfect. Being as how I was getting closer to Mexico with every stride I figured to keep it. I carried it back under my arm, wearing my own beat up felt as I didn't want to be mistaken for a bandit by those in the adobe who might be a little nervous and trigger-happy.

All of them were gathered around the gold and paper money on the table, chattering in wonder as I entered. "Don't be admiring it too much," I said with some authority. "It's going to Maricopa Wells with me. Some of it was stolen from me, most from other folks."

Then I turned to Tobias, who was now prone on an upholstered love seat against the far wall. "The Concord is turning around and going back to Maricopa Wells. And you need to get to the doc there. Can you instruct these fellows how to rig up that four up—"

"We have to go on," Mr. Kirby-Jones said.

"And you will, after I get Tobias to the doc

and this stolen loot and the bodies to Maricopa Wells."

Tobias started to answer, but his son Thomas stepped forward. "I can rig it. I help pa twice a day."

"Hold up now," the stage whip, Cajun Jesse, stepped forward. "I got a schedule to keep. We'll be headin' on."

And Kirby-Jones chimed in again, "That's a fact. We gotta—"

My anger was palpable. "You gotta help save the life of this man who was wounded keeping y'all safe. If'n you want to keep the gunfire going, argue with me." I gave the whip a stiff finger in the chest. "Besides, a good deal of this loot likely belongs to Wells Fargo and others. It doesn't get safe returned, Jesse, I'll let it be known that's on you."

None of them said a word.

Then Cajun Jesse spoke up and Moony nodded. "We'll lend a hand. Looks like enough critters to fill the six-up harness. If we're gonna use raw stock, might as well train 'em all."

"Lend a hand harnessing and loading these three bodies on the roof of the coach."

Kirby-Jones complained, "Why bother. Let the buzzards have 'em."

Again my tone wasn't friendly. "Because they're worth money to me, that's why. I didn't ride into this gunfight just to save your hide. Now let's get moving." I turned to Mrs. Magruder. "Ma'am, it's another thirty miles to Maricopa Wells. We should eat, then I suggest you close up and y'all come with us. Those Apache raiders could return."

"Well, sir," she replied, "supper I'll do, but then we three Magruders will stay on and do our job. We'll have another stage roll in coming from Wickenburg and them folks will need to eat and the stock rest up as there'll be no fresh team."

"Your decision ma'am, but I'd—"

She stopped me short. "That's right, my decision. Now get moving and get Mr. Magruder to the doc. Have Wells Fargo send a couple of folks out to do our job and with a fresh team then we'll ride in."

Dang if this country doesn't breed tough folks. I shook my head in amazement as we all got to work. It would likely be a heck of a wild trip with a mix of horses and mules, some never in harness. But the Concord was the only way to get Tobias to a doc and expect him to live the trip.

I informed them as neither the gray nor the roan had been in harness, and likely not the chestnut, I intended to have him for myself. Besides a stallion, which I believed him to be, would likely never team up well. I dragged the gray and the roan, them packed with the loot and vittles. The Kirby-Jones couple was again inside, Tobias prone across from them and Cade Tolliver, Lucas "Dutch" Van Horn and Carlos Apeza tied atop and dead as yesterday, we sat off. Cajun Jesse was the whip and Moony Williams the shotgun on the high seat.

Now, if only the Apache had disappeared deep into the Gila Bends, the Big Horns, or the Buckeye Mountains, we'd likely make Maricopa Wells safely.

Likely, but nothing was for sure in this wild country.

Chapter Twenty-Seven

MacGillicutty's River Station was on a low rise two hundred yards from the wide but shallow Gila River. The station mistress was a gruff unfriendly red-headed woman and the master equally grumpy, with a belly that had kept him from seeing his feet for many years and with hair and beard as black as a foot up a bull's butt. In fact he smelled as if he'd been there. We finally talked him into taking the six head pulling the Concord for four broke to harness, and rolled on the next eighteen miles into Maricopa Wells.

I insisted we drive straight to the docs, unloaded Tobias, then to the federal marshal's office. He was out the door almost before the coach stopped rolling.

"What the devil do we have here?" he asked, hands on hips, eyeing the load atop the stage.

Dismounting, throwing the heavy neck bags over a shoulder, I strode over and extended a hand, which he took. "Let's talk private," I said.

"And who might you be?" he asked, eyeing me skeptically.

"Let's talk inside. It's a long story."

He nodded, then turned and I followed him in.

There was a deputy standing in the doorway, who followed us through an outer office into the marshal's.

"Nothing personal," I said, nodding to the deputy, "but let's keep this between you and me."

The marshal shrugged and snapped at the deputy, "Morgan, give us some privacy. Then he turned to me, "Coffee?"

"Yes, sir. Obliged."

After I fished out ten twenty dollar gold pieces—expenses—I dropped the neck bags on his desk with a heavy plop. As he walked over and yelled out his office door for two cups of coffee, I informed him, "This is just some of the ill-gotten gains of the Cade Tolliver gang, much of it mine. I'm delivering him, Lucas "Dutch" Van Horn and Carlos Apaza, and claiming the reward for them.

I believe the flyers say dead or alive. And back up the trail some forty miles I can direct you to the body of Billy Bob Ten Gauge, if the critters ain't et him, I am claiming that reward as well."

He returned with two cups of steaming coffee in hand and plopped down in his chair, was quiet for a moment then asked, "Who the hell are you and how old are you?"

I couldn't help but smile, then answered, "I don't want it advertised, which is the reason I wanted to talk alone. My real name is Conn Donahey but my non-de-plume is Conn Callihan. I'll be twenty in a few weeks."

"Why the phony name?"

"A friend of mine advised me that a fella didn't want to get a reputation if he didn't want other fellas trying to make theirs off of filling him full of holes."

The sheriff laughed a little at that. "I guess that be sound advice. I'll keep the Donahey to myself."

"Obliged. Now, let's count this bag full so I can get a receipt from you."

Now he yelled at his deputy. "Mathieson, get in here and bring something to write on."

The bags held some little more than eight thousand dollars in gold coins comprised of over three hundred fifty twenty-dollar liberty head gold pieces plus miscellaneous, twenty-six pounds of gold bars at eighteen dollars and ninety-four cents the ounce or seventy-eight hundred or so and sixty-one thousand dollars in paper money, even discounted it would amount to over thirty thousand dollars. At the minimum the bags carried over forty-five thousand in value. In addition there was a bag full of jewelry which we described but had no idea its value. The sheriff said there was a knowledgeable jeweler in town and he would call on him for an appraisal.

I did inform the sheriff and placed in writing a claim on three thousand dollars of the recovered loot, Sarah Ann's twenty-five hundred dowry and five hundred of the twelve hundred proceeds of the sale of Fenton's Forge, the portion I hadn't kept in my saddlebag and boot.

A little gobsmacked I sat back in my chair when he informed me the reward offered by the territorial governor was ten percent of any recovered loot, and that for merely giving information leading to its recovery. I had yet to mention I knew the location of a buried trunk, likely under tons of rock, with, God only knows, how much more loot. If my friend Hector hadn't returned with pick and shovel and a dozen Chinese miners to claim it.

It was only then I asked, "Have you seen a rider with a woman in tow, both of them Mexican, the woman likely bound so she can't escape?"

"If anyone in this town saw a man dragging a woman bound...well if they didn't shoot him in the brisket they'd at least come running."

"Then if they came this way, they likely stayed clear of town. Word is they're headed for Mexico."

"Half the territory is headed for a new town being called Tombstone. If not Mexico, then Tombstone. Been cattle country for decades but now mining country as well. Like all boomtowns I hear it's attracting every owlhoot, grifter, crooked gambler and road agent from this and other territories. Behan's the sheriff there. Tell him you're a friend of mine."

I chewed on that a moment, then asked, "Where and how far is this Tombstone?"

"A good piece, maybe one hundred and seventy-five miles. You keep heading for Tucson, which will take you closer to Mexico, then a good ways beyond."

"Then I'm headed for Tombstone."

"First head over to Maricopa Bank and Safe

Holding Company and open an account. When your reward is cleared, your money will be there."

I shook his hand. "When I return, I'll buy you the biggest steak in town."

"Mexican Bob is a mean hombre, half gila monster half rattlesnake. What do we do with your money you don't return?"

"I'll be back, but if not two thousand five hundred dollars goes to Seth Macintosh on the Bar Five just outside of Prescott." I thought for a moment, then remembered my brother and sister who I hadn't seen in over five years. "I got a brother Hugh and sister Fiona. Last I heard of them, they were living in St. Louis with our uncle and aunt, Sean and Sophie Callihan."

"You got time for that steak now? You can dictate your intentions...I guess your will...to Mathieson on the way out and he'll have it writ up by the time we return."

"Sounds fine as frog hair, then after we put that steak away and I open that account I could use a bath, haircut, and a shave."

"McBride's has the best steak in the territory, let's go."

A half day's rest and then three, maybe four, days of hard riding and, God willing, a little luck, my quest will end.

Chapter Twenty-Eight

Well fed and refreshed, riding the chestnut and leaving the gray and the roan in a Maricopa Wells livery to rest up, we made good time. I also left the 73 with the sheriff for safekeeping as I didn't want to load the chestnut down. I took only my bedroll and jerky and hardtack for three days...and, of course my Sharps and coach gun, my bear trap, now two belly guns, and the Remington Frontier Single Action Army and stag handle knife I'd taken off Apaza.

The country was nearly flat with some great small-town-size castle rocks poking up out of the desert for scenery, and water at every stage station along the way. The chestnut and I put three and a half stations behind us by the middle of the second day then stopped for a sit-down meal and grain for the chestnut at the forth on the outskirts of Tucson. The station master informed me I was over halfway and had some seventy-five miles to go.

The mistress of the station was a talker and educated me that a hundred years before Tucson was a Mexican outpost, a one hundred seventy-five-foot square with three-foot-thick abode walls, walled in town housing *soldados* and a church, but now the railroad has arrived and it's a blooming city of commerce. The new Pima County Bank was the most impressive structure in town, even though Tucson was yet to have any paving or streetlights. I admired the city fathers as they'd adopted a homestead plan. You could acquire a city lot for free so long as you did one hundred dollars in improvements. Made me wish I had time to hang around.

After forking over four bits for a steak—my suspicions it was burro as it chewed like boot leather—but the peach cobbler was worth the money, I headed into town hoping I wasn't too late for a bath and shave. And I wanted to see the sights and treat myself to a beer.

And I kept it to one beer, paying the local hostler four bits for graining and stalling the chestnut and another two bits for me sleeping in the hayloft. Rather than pay for a bath, he let me douse in the horse trough. Without hot water I passed on the shave.

Well rested, the chestnut was pounding trail well before the sun colored the mountains to the east and by early afternoon, we reined up in front of the second stage stop out of Tucson on the road to Tombstone. A couple of Italian brothers ran the place and kept a big kettle of soup hot at all times, a bowl of that, some great hard bread, a glass of red wine, a quarter nose bag of grain for the chestnut and we were off again. With only twenty miles to go, the last station before Tombstone, we talked them out of a late supper and were off again before sunrise.

The railroad had just been completed from Tucson to Tombstone but I wanted the chestnut with me and he wouldn't ride well in a stock car with others, so passed on the easy way.

All along the way I'd inquired about Mexican Bob and Elena, and feared I was on the wrong trail as I got no positive responses. My first instinct was to head straight south out of Maricopa Wells. I guess I'll soon find out if I should have followed my instinct.

The discovery of silver and the Tombstone

Mine has driven the boomtown to near a thousand occupants, and growing so fast they couldn't be counted. Most residents were living in tents, wagons, mesquite wickiups, or merely under blankets…but wooden structures were rising fast even though lumber had to be hauled all the way from the Huachuca Mountains.

As always, saloons and gambling houses were leading the way. The town was isolated on a mile-high ledge of bedrock—the altitude made for decent cool nights—in the heart of a great desert, the Mule and Dragoon Mountains in sight. Stamp mills were already under construction in the near San Pedro Valley where there was abundant water, and the town of Charleston was rising around them. It was in a contest with Tombstone for most lawless.

And danged if Tombstone wasn't the strangest town I'd ever seen. The whole town was mining claims, as was the desert beyond. Dead center in a street called Toughnut gaped a forty-foot long, twenty-foot wide, now twenty-foot deep, hole that sported a guard at each end every night. Word was a fortune in silver ore was being dug from that hole during the daylight hours and lanterns lit the hole at night to guard against thieves. And it wasn't the only unban mine. I was

advised to be careful with my footing or I'd disappear into a shaft.

I was also advised by the hostler, Farley
O'Toole, who charged me the outrageous sum of
a dollar a night for the chestnut...and I was not
invited to sleep in the hayloft...but the advice was
free. The advice was to steer clear of those boys
with the red sashes around their waist, who called
themselves cowboys. I got a quick history, of the
area, from cow country to mining country, mostly
under the control of a fella who claimed to be a
cattleman but who'd built his herds rustling from
others. He called himself Old Man Clanton and
had three sons Joseph Isaac, who went by Ike;
Phineas, who went by Phin; and William who
went by Billy. All known to be outlaws following
in daddy's footsteps. And the old man was
followed by, and Farley advised me to put the
names to memory: Curly Bill Brocius, John Ringo,
Frank and Tom McLowery, Joe Hill, Jim Hughes,
Pony Deal, Frank Stilwell and Pete Spence. Then
he shocked me with "how many more than two
hundred cowboy bandits claiming allegiance to
Clanton there is I can't guess."

"And the law?" I asked.

"You swear on your ma's grave you won't
repeat me?"

"Hell, I already forgot your name and what you look like."

He laughed a little then continued, "There ain't none. Johnny Behan, a no-good low life self-serving son of a bitch poses as if he's the law...but word is Wyatt Earp and his family, wives, brothers, is coming to town. It's said Wyatt cleaned up Dodge City, Wichita, Ellsworth and Abilene. Maybe he can get things right."

I shook my head in doubt. "I met brother Virgil in Prescott. But two or three fellas again' two hundred or more. I wouldn't bet the farm...."

"One can only pray."

Then I went on to ask, "You ever hear of a Mexican Bob?"

He shrugged.

So, I continued, "Another no-good, likely make your Behan look like Gabriel the angel. He's rumored to be heading for Mexico but if there's easy pickin's hereabout he might hang on here to add to his purse. He's traveling with a Mexican lady, light-skinned, beautiful, lips red as a cactus flower, raven-wing black hair to a waist you could circle with your hands, and she's likely trying to fight shy of his company if possible. He left from up near Wickenburg with her tied to the saddle horn. Mexican Bob has a slash of white hair among the black...but he seldom is without a brown sombrero with a band of silver coins."

"What's your interest in this Mexican Bob?"

"On your ma's grave?"

"Just like you swore."

"He was with a bunch who killed my wife of just a few hours may have fired the shot. A lady as beautiful as a mountain meadow full of wildflowers and with a spirit as pure as spring water and I mean to avenge her...and won't rest until I do. He was one of nine, now he's one alone."

"And you settled with them eight?"

"I did, and I have one to go. Along the way, I am gonna return Miss Elena to her rightful home."

"Mexicans hang out in a cantina made of mesquite, Café Corazon, not much more than a wickiup, about a mile south of the last claim. But watch yourself there as a fella could get a machete splittin' his skull should he have a ha'penny one of them greasers took a shine to."

"I do believe I'll wander out that way."

"Keep your back to the wall."

"It's come to be a habit. I thank you for the enlightenment. Should I see you in the saloon, it's good whiskey on me."

"Speakin' of saloons, I should have mentioned

The Charleston, right in the center of town, is where the riffraff in red sashes hang out...sometimes the Occidental. Be careful at the Corazon, but double careful at The Charleston and Occidental. Most the customers there have left bodies behind like spits of chaw. And back shootin' is a fair fight to them."

Curious, I asked, "So was the nearby town named for the saloon or vice versa?"

"Charleston was named for its postmaster and there's Millville right across the river. No idee why the saloon."

"I'll be back to stall the chestnut."

"You will if you keep your back to the wall."

Chapter Twenty-Nine

We took our time passing through Tombstone, dodging drays, freight wagons, ore wagons, other horsebackers and pedestrians crossing the streets ankle deep in dust.

The Cochise County Bank caught my eye and set me to thinking, boomtowns offer lots of opportunity, but opportunity is fueled by money and rather than risk carrying a lot with me I'd left most of my worth at the Maricopa Bank and Safe Holding Company, which should be about to receive a lot more in the way of rewards. I hitched up outside the two-story building, dug the five hundred in gold coin I had with me out of my saddlebag and entered, only to stand in line.

I opened an account with four hundred fifty

and asked to see the manager, and was led to an office in the rear and introduced to Angus Campbell-Stuart. He didn't bother to rise or extend a hand. Angus was a stout fellow with a fine suit of clothes but the coat hung on a nearby rack and his sleeves were rolled up, collar loosened, and waistcoat unbuttoned. His sideburns, flanking a round head shiny bald on top, were full to the jawbone yet his chin shaved clean.

And he wasn't one to dillydally. "What's your business, young man?"

"I'd like to transfer some money from the Maricopa Bank."

He eyed me up and down and snapped, "Don't do transfers less than a hundred dollars and charge five percent at that."

I admit I looked like I didn't have a farthing much less more than a hundred dollars. Deciding I'd get his attention, I informed him, "I just opened an account with four hundred fifty in gold, so that should stand for something. Now, does the fee go down if the transfer is more?"

He studied me for a moment. "Will do four percent for a thousand."

"A thousand sounds fine but I'll only pay two percent."

Again he studied me. "Three and a half is low as I'll go."

"Three is a deal. There will be more to come should I decide to set up shop here."

"And what's your business?"

"I'm a smithy. Sold my forge in Prescott."

"Three and a quarter is my bottom dollar."

"And the bank guarantee's arrival."

"Not for three and a quarter percent we don't. You want a guarantee it's ten percent and we have thirty days to pay up."

"I'll take my chances with three and a quarter."

I composed a telegram to Maricopa Wells to the Maricopa Bank and Safe Holding Company explaining, in addition to my deposit, my reward due, advising the bank to check with the sheriff. Offering to pay the loan rate of two percent per month I knew them to be charging until my funds arrived, should they not already be there. I wandered the streets for an hour awaiting the reply and left for the cantina knowing I had a thousand in gold coming on the next stage. Angus the banker was much more the polite businessman when I took my leave.

The cantina was easy to find, and thirty paces behind it was an adobe house, and beyond it a barn. A dozen horses were tied at rails outside the Corazon. The strumming of a guitar, well played, welcomed me as I entered with Sharps in one hand and coach gun hanging from the other. I wore Apaza's sombrero pulled low. Six tables held from one to four customers each and four fellas leaned on a bar that would accommodate a dozen. The guitar player sat at a table with others and two barmaids worked the room, one couldn't have been more than twelve, the other had been at tortillas made from lard and filled with *frijoles* for too many years. She wore a single braid so long it rested on her generous butt. I moved quickly to a far end of the bar and leaned the long arms beneath. As Mexican Bob might recognize me, I quickly surveyed the place then—ignoring my promise—gave them my back as the bartender came my way.

"What you have, *gringo*?" he asked.

I guess the sombrero fooled no one. "Pulque and some information."

"Pulque is two bits. Information? Price depends..."

I shrugged. "Just looking for a friend. He came down from Prescott and asked me to join him."

"This *amigo*, he has a name?"

"He does, a proud one. Roberto Camacho... some call him Mexican Bob."

"You the law—"

I laughed, then pulled the coach gun up high enough he could see. My tone changed to half growl. "Pick one of those *caballeros* you want me to beat to a pulp or fill full of buckshot and I'll prove I ain't the law."

He had a bottle of pulque in one hand but held the other toward me, palm out. "Hold on, no killing the customers. Like I said, information is very valuable. You got a ten-dollar gold piece?"

"I got two two-dollar gold pieces, but should I get bad information I might return."

This time it was he who shrugged. "I can only speak of yesterday."

"Yesterday will do," I said, slapping the two gold coins on the bar.

"And two bits for the pulque." So, I added the coin.

He surveyed the saloon as if he didn't want anyone to overhear him giving a stranger information, which gave me come confidence.

He spoke in low tones. "Mexican Bob was looking for some *banditos* to tie up with. I sent him to see *Señor Hombre Viejo* Clanton...Old Man Clanton."

"Did Comacho have a woman with him?"

He studied me for a moment. "You said you sought Roberto Camacho?"

"I do, but the woman means something to me."

"Another dollar?"

I felt like busting his nose with the butt of the coach gun, but it came to me not to lose sight of my objective. I fished out another dollar.

"While Comacho drank, his woman went out back with my señora and her clothes were washed and she bathed. They had supper in my casa then left to ride to the Clanton's. She told *mi esposa* she wanted to get away from Comacho, but *mi esposa* told her it was not our business. So they rode on."

"To where?"

"Lewis Springs. Up the Rio San Pedro above Charleston and Millville."

"How far, and how many men does Clanton have around?"

"Ten miles to Charleston, maybe *dos mas* to Lewis Springs. How many *hombres*? Maybe ten, maybe a hundred."

As I rode out, I wondered, nine enemies is one thing, a hundred another altogether.

Chapter Thirty

No more than back on the road, heading southwest, I fell in behind a train of ore wagons. Three sets of two, each being pulled by mules, ten-hitch teams. The elevation of Tombstone, or so I'm told, is just over four thousand feet and Charleston just under so the trip was fairly easy.

I've paid little attention to the date but it must be June, and the temperature is now over one hundred degrees in the heat of the day. The country is greasewood without much mesquite, so very little shade, and I want to get to the river and hopefully some shade before the heat of the day, so I pick up the pace and pass the three sets of wagons. As the day wears on the mesquite thickens and finally I spot a thick row of cottonwood, and as suspected, the San Pedro River. Thankfully it runs clear. I've just passed a cutoff, plain to see that's the way the heavy wagons follow, but a small sign points on the less used branch of the road. The sign was so worn I had to dismount to read **Lewis Springs 2 Miles**.

As I don't know what I'm riding into, after following the road on the Lewis Springs side, I rein off until I find a good stand of graze for the chestnut near the clear flowing river, dismount and drop his saddle and stake him with only a lead rope. I'm near enough the road—in deep shade so I likely can't be seen—I watch the three sets of wagons as they rumble by and take The Charleston branch a hundred yards back. I'm about to doze off using the saddle to lean against, when above the trickle of the river I hear laughter. The chestnut is in heavy brush so he's out of sight as well.

Keeping my eyes glued on the road, four riders come into view, moving along two by two at an easy walk. When near enough, maybe forty yards, I decide it not wise to yell a greeting...all four wear the red sashes of the cowboy gang.

As I don't know the location of the Clanton spread I'm tempted to follow but don't. Rather I let the chestnut rest until damn near sundown.

Then I fish my little pot out of a bag and my pan and slice and fry up some side pork and enjoy it and the soppin's with some hardtack. Topped off with a couple of tin cups of coffee.

I'm forking out the last slice of side pork when I'm startled by a voice, "Howdy the camp."

With my Colt in hand, I yell back, "It's a welcome camp, come on in." And out of the brush stride two fellas, cowboys, but they stop short.

The taller of the two has his hand on his revolver as he asks, "You gonna put that iron back to bed?"

"Sorry, a fella can't be too careful." And I holster the weapon.

"Any coffee to spare?" the shorter one asks.

"Not brewed, but we got plenty of water and I ground up lots before I set out."

"Set out for where?" the tall one asks.

I'm thinking fast, so as I'm digging for my pouch of ground coffee, lie, "An old doc back in Tucson told me Lewis Springs could help a fella's ills should he soak there a few days. So, I'm headed there."

I get the pot back on the fire and only then stick out a hand, "I'm Callihan, and you?"

The stocky one took the hand and shook. "Dave, and that's Tom."

I nod, as if that's enough, then add, "Where you fellas headed?"

"The Clanton outfit. Best you stop by and Howdy Old Man Clanton. He'll be wanting a dollar a day you use the spring."

"Dang, that's pretty proud for a soak."

"Price is what it is. Old Man Clanton ran the Apache out of this country so it would have cost you your hair before. Guess he can set his price."

"Guess he can," I said with a shake of the head. "I may just pass on the spring as a dollar would about bust me, and head back to Tombstone."

"We're headed to Clanton's and you're welcome to ride in with us."

"Thanks, but if a soak's a dollar, I can't afford to scrub my hands."

They downed some coffee, having to dig their own cups out, then the one called Tom eyed my saddle on the ground and asked, "Where's your nag?"

As I'd seemed to have convinced them I wasn't worth robbing, the last thing I wanted to do was have them see the chestnut. "Poor old mare is on her last legs. Rode her all the way from

Prescott and had to catch a ride on an ore wagon draggin' her to get this far. I may be on shanks mare from here on." I could see Tom didn't believe me.

Then the one called himself Dave spoke up, "We're gonna miss supper. Let's get our ass down the trail."

Tom eyed me, then noticed the butt of the Sharps in its scabbard. Dave followed his line of sight and I slipped my Colts out.

They turned back to me. "That's a Sharps?"

I cocked the Colt. "It is, forty-five-ninety, and I'm keeping it."

Tom shrugged. "Nobody said you wasn't. Thanks for the coffee." They took a few steps away and I slipped the coach gun out and cocked it as they spun back, reaching for their sidearms. They seemed surprised to be facing the cocked scattergun in one hand and my Colt in the other.

Both of them let their revolvers slip back. "You're a suspicious sort," Dave said, it was just light enough to see the evil smile he wore.

I nodded. "Seems for good reason. This scattergun is good for close work and if someone decides they be interested in my goods, the Sharps has been known to hit a dinner plate at three hundred yards...with me on the sights, of course. You fellas have a good ride to the Clanton's place."

"Maybe see you in Tombstone," Dave yelled back over his shoulder, his tone sarcastic.

They disappeared into the brush. I quickly kicked dirt on the fire and in the dark broke camp, retrieved and packed the chestnut, and set out to follow Dave and Tom, but riding with the scattergun across my thighs.

I figured I'd gone less than three miles when I saw the lights from windows more than a quarter mile ahead.

There was a long low rise behind the place and I reined the chestnut up the hill until I figured I was at least a quarter mile behind and above the ranch buildings. Finding a place reasonable flat with a bit of graze, where I could not see lights of the ranch, I unloaded and made a dry camp.

Tomorrow should be an interesting day.

Chapter Thirty-One

It wasn't the best night's sleep I ever enjoyed. The coyotes sounded close enough to hit with a rock and the wind blew like it wanted to push me back to Prescott. Dry lightning lit the sky and at times thunder rolled long and low until I wondered if it would ever stop, but we were blessed with no monsoon or nary a drop of rain. I feared making a fire so breakfast was jerky and hardtack washed down with San Pedro River water with which I'd filled my canteen.

I repacked and moved through the mesquite down within three hundred yards of the ranch buildings where an outcropping of sandstone allowed me to get some height and climbed up and bellied down to watch the comings and goings of the Clanton Ranch.

The house was fair size, adobe and one story, but large enough for four bedrooms. The barn could have held a dozen stalls and the loft several tons of loose hay. Beyond but attached to the barn were two large corrals, one the remuda of horses with at least three dozen head and the other divided into two, one with bull calves or steers likely for butchering and another much smaller, surrounded with three-foot uprights of mesquite less than six inches apart held a half dozen snorting hogs. Three outbuildings seemed first to be a forge—it a log structure—and two bunkhouses, also adobe. There was also a small plank privy between the bunkhouses and another just back of the house. Nearer the house was a hand pump which meant the water table was likely no more than ten or fifteen feet. The main house was shaded by two large cottonwoods and tables and benches sat in their shade.

Watching and trying to keep track at least a dozen came and went to and from the privies, then about seven a.m., an hour after dawn, a Chinaman exited the house and beat an iron triangle, the cowboys filtered out of the barn and bunkhouses and gathered at the tables. The

Chinaman, a couple of chubby Mexican girls, and to my surprise, a slender girl began serving the cowboys. From the distance I couldn't be positive, but were I a betting man I'd have bet my dollar against a dime it was Elena.

I studied them at the table, now easily counting fourteen, but with half of them wearing sombreros could not determine which, if any, might be Mexican Bob.

Knowing I had to get closer, I backed down off my perch and worked my way through the mesquite until I had a good view of the corrals. And, sure enough, among the stock was a palomino mare with lots of white in her coat, a blaze on her nose, and white stockings. The horse Elena had been riding.

As I sat in the shade of a sandstone ledge studying the remuda I also picked out the black Mexican Bob rode.

Then I began to wonder. If I wasn't mistaken, the girl I thought to be Elena had been laughing and chattering with the cowboys. Could it be she had no interest in being rescued? That thought threw a whole new light on things. The fact could be she was now taken with Bob. He was a tall handsome Mexican, even if a lowlife crook who'd likely kill his grandmother for a tortilla. Hell, stranger things had happened.

But no matter, I meant to kill Mexican Bob and if Elena didn't want to return to her adopted parents, so be it. Her choice.

I guess I shouldn't have been daydreaming, with my scattergun across my thighs, as a gruff voice snapped me back to reality.

"You lay a hand on that Colt and you're a dead man." I whipped my head to the left and was staring into the barrel of a revolver.

"And he don't miss and neither to I," and I whipped my gaze to the right to see an equally large barrel aimed about head high.

The fellow on my left dropped a loop over me as I looked right and sucked it up tight. Then he asked, "What the hell are you doing?"

I smiled at him. "I was just trying to figure out if I'd be welcome for breakfast?"

He laughed as the other one dropped another loop over me, then he answered my question. "Breakfast? Sure, you'll be welcome...welcome as breakfast for them hogs down yonder."

After relieving me of my Colt—luckily I'd laid the scattergun in a bushy greasewood—they started dragging me, stumbling, away from my shadowed hideout under the sandstone, leaving my scattergun behind. Their horses were tied at about forty yards and they mounted up and heeled them into a trot. I tried desperately to keep my feet but hit the ground and bounced from mesquite to mesquite and plowed grease-wood with my head and shoulders.

I was near unconscious when they dismounted and recovered their reatas, then a bucket of water hit me in the face and I shook my head until semi-conscious. I was staring into the pocked face of an old man with a shock of gray hair. He was leaning over me, hands on his knees. Then I realized a half dozen stood around behind him, eyeballing me.

He spat a stream of tobacco near me, then asked, "You with the cattlemen's association, a federal marshal, a county sheriff's deputy, or just a common thief looking to see what you can steal?"

I tried to muster a smile but found it difficult with a mouth full of desert rock and sand. Managing to answer, I first spit out some dirt and gravel. "I'm just a passerby wondering if you had work or could spare a meal for a hungry pilgrim."

I glanced over to see another cowboy leading the chestnut.

The old man sneered at me. "Damn nice mount and rig for a hungry pilgrim. A fine Sharps, a Colt and a Remington, a couple of belly guns, a damn bear trap that would take your leg off, and a fat handful of gold coin. Who the hell are you?"

I was silent for a moment, then the old man kicked me in the side hard enough I worried he might have broken a rib, so I spoke up. "Word was y'all could use a gun in your line of business and it was profitable to tie in with the cowboys. I'm more'n a fair hand with all that iron, should that be the case."

"You ain't the law?"

"You see a badge on me?"

"Don't mean nothing."

"I presume you're Old Man Clanton...who I came to see. Give me one of my weapons, any one of them, and I'll prove you can use me."

"Not likely. We got a hole to put you in 'til I decide what to do with you." Then he turned to the others. "Put this snoop in the guest house."

As they dragged me away, I caught a glimpse of Elena and know she recognized me, but it gave me hope as she did not call out or say anything.

Turns out the guest house was a cave with bars of heavy mesquite spaced only six inches apart. The cave was only six feet deep and barely tall enough to stand up in. They placed two buckets inside before chaining up and walking away. One of the buckets was filled with water, one empty which I presumed was my toilet. I shook the bars and decided they were buried two feet deep and mortared in the top. The chain and lock were heavy. By the stench and trash I figured I wasn't the first house guest.

I had not seen Mexican Bob and wondered if he'd recognize me if he looked me in the eye. I knew Elena had.

Now, the problem was, get the hell out of this hole, get my gear back, get Mexican Bob dead as a hob nail, and get on the road with Elena should she want to go.

Other than that, no problem.

Chapter Thirty-Two

I had a hell of a time trying to sleep. The ribs the old man had kicked pained me something terrible and I prayed they weren't broken. Ribs took a long time to heal. And it was damn hot in the cave.

The fat Mexican woman I'd seen serving the men at the outside table showed up with a bowl of frijoles and shoved them under the gate with a wooden spoon and motioned for me to put the water bucket up next to the mesquite bars. I did and she managed to fill it from a large pitcher, then left without a word.

Night fell and I welcomed the cooler weather, and was finally dozing when I heard, or sensed, quiet footfalls.

Then, "Conn...Conn, it's Elena."

"Good to see you're okay," I said, my face against the bars.

"Did you come to help me escape?"

"I did, and to settle with Mexican Bob."

"I have your horse and mine saddled. I took a reata off another saddle. Do you think my mare can pull the gate open?"

"Only one way to find out," I said. "Give me an end. Keep the loop for your saddle horn."

The hinge on the gate was of thick bull leather, almost the length of the gate and nailed on the outside. I tied the reata around the bar nearest the hinge thinking it might give way.

Elena mounted, riding like a man with her full skirt, keeping the reata under her leg and next to the saddle, and moved the palomino forward until there was a strain on the line, but even kicking the mare's ribs, nothing gave way.

She dismounted and walked back near so we could whisper.

"I am so sorry, Conn, I hoped—"

"Bring her back so you can get a run at it."

"I've come to love my palomino. Are you sure it will not injure—"

"She's tough, she'll be fine, and Mexican Bob may injure you far worse."

"He's already threatened to give me to the others if I don't mind."

"Let's get out of here."

She repositioned the mare so she could get a twenty-foot run at it, and this time gigged the horse hard. She almost came over backward when she hit the end of the line, and Elena screamed a little.

I prayed no one heard but even more so that I could fit through the space made by the broken mesquite. It hadn't pulled the hinge loose but busted the rail it was tied to. I kicked away the remnants and squeezed through.

After checking the cinch on the chestnut, I mounted, then waved Elena up beside me. "The old man has my saddlebags and weapons. Where would they be?"

"I must escape, Conn. I cannot wait—"

"No need for you to wait. Walk your horse until at least a hundred yards away. Then lope if you can for a while."

"I could gallop all night if it meant getting away from that pig."

"Where are my goods?"

"There's a bedroom at the far end of the house. Outside it is a room he uses for an office.

There's a safe there and some gun racks. I would guess there."

"Get moving. If you hear someone coming, hide off the trail...and if you make Tombstone go to the livery and ask Farley O'Toole, who owns the place, to help out. Tomorrow if I haven't shown up go to the Cochise County Bank and see Angus Campbell-Stuart, the manager. Tell him I said give you two hundred dollars. I have money there, my special word for the account is Rumpelstiltskin and the amount is four hundred fifty dollars in the account, with more to come. No one else will know that and he should give you no trouble. Now go."

And she did, walking the mare.

I had a hunch, so I reined the chestnut back up the hill until I found the ledge I'd hidden under, where I'd been discovered. I rustled around under the brush and as I suspected they hadn't found the coach gun I'd dropped in some greasewood.

Then I returned and tied the chestnut near the back door and was not surprised when it was not locked. I made my way through the kitchen, a dining room, a great room and down a hall until it opened into a room with desk and safe, and a door to what I guessed was the old man's private bedroom. He had the trappings of a cattle king even though he was the king of thieves.

The place was rough, not fancy, but roomy.

The moon was up and near full and some light lit the room from a large window behind the desk. Sure as hell my saddle bags hung over the chair behind his desk, my Sharps was in the rack with a dozen other rifles, my Colt and Remington on pegs in the wall nearby among others, but my belly guns were nowhere to be seen. However, among several handguns on the pegs was a fine two-barrel Derringer. It would do just fine.

Over my shoulder went the bags, in a trouser pocket, the Derringer, and I carried a long arm in each hand. I almost got out without seeing my newly acquired sombrero on a rack near the door, but leaned the Sharps on the wall and donned the hat.

Loaded down, I moved quietly back through the house to the back door, and fidgeted around to open it, only to suddenly come face to face, eye to eye, with a fella my big who was outside reaching for the latch.

He managed to utter a "What..."

I handed him the Sharps. "Hold this."

He did, all the while trying to figure out who and what, as I jerked the Remington from my belt and hit him alongside the head so hard it would likely be a week before he came to.

I moved quickly to the chestnut. Pleased to find the scabbards still in place, I fixed the saddle-bags behind the saddle and rode out at a slow quiet pace.

When clear of earshot, I gigged the big horse into a lope. Two miles and I came to the fork with one branch going to Charleston and one on to Tombstone. I barely got past the fork when a voice rang out. "Conn...Conn Donahey!"

I reined up and Elena appeared out of a thick stand of mesquite.

"You're easy to spot with that white mane and tail."

"Please, I'm now known as Conn Callihan. Donahey is my past."

"As you wish, Conn Callihan."

"Let's get moving," I said, and we did, at a lope for at least three of the ten miles left.

Tombstone was coming alive as we entered at a brisk walk.

Chapter Thirty-Three

The Grand Hotel was accepting guests and Elena followed me into the lobby where the desk man was asleep in a chair with his feet up on another.

I rapped on the counter, waking him.

"Sir, a room for the lady. Do you offer bathing facilities?"

He bellied up to the counter and adjusted his pince-nez glasses, grabbed a pencil, and studied a journal. Then he asked, "Just the lady? You won't be joining her."

"Just the lady and a bath."

"The room is a dollar and a quarter a night, eight dollars the week. The bath, in the room in our leather tub, another six bits."

"That's proud for a bath?"

"Hot water, lugged up them stairs a pair of buckets at a time? I'd say it's a fine price."

"Let's get the lady a room for the night and a bath at her pleasure. Listen close, the lady has some want to do her harm. It would serve you well no one knows she's here...under your protection and I'd take it personal should harm come to her."

He eyed us both carefully then asked, "It ain't the law involved?"

"No, sir, my word. It's personal business."

He gave me a satisfied nod.

I paid the man two bucks, then turned to Elena. "Walk me to the door." And she did. In a low voice, I asked, "I know you've had a hard few days. Please, don't show your face on the street or even in the restaurant. We'll have breakfast brought up. I'm off to the bank to get you some money and to the stage station to book you home to the Johansons."

She began to cry. Then blubbered, "How can I repay—"

"You home safe is payment enough. Anna was kind to me, and this is repayment to her." I offered her my neckerchief from my back pocket.

"Why don't you come—"

"I have business here. I'll never rest until Mexican Bob has dirt in his face."

"Bob robbed you?"

"Bob was with them that murdered my wife... my wife of six hours. The worms will have him before I rest."

I walked her back to the desk, paid him four bits for her breakfast and another dime tip, and excused myself.

Before giving the town the once over, I picked up a copy of each of the two newspapers, *The Nugget*, which seemed on the side of the outlaw red-sash segment; and The Epitaph, which supported town folk and those in favor of law and order. I was amused by an article that stated Tombstone was becoming known for having "A man for breakfast every day," or otherwise at least one man was gunned down every night.

I spent the rest of the day getting familiar with the town.

Wandering in and out of the Occidental, Ayer's Saloon, The Charleston, Hafford's Bar and the Cosmopolitan, I was half glad it was before lunch as even then some of the faro and poker tables were full, and by the looks of the players many had been there from last night. Doc Holliday's admonition of "keep your back to the wall" seemed born of such places, and he was an expert in their machinations and risks.

Finding a tonsorial parlor I stopped in and first took advantage of the bath in the back, then a shave and trim in the front. Another dollar lightened my purse.

It was clear to me that Mexican Bob had tied up with Clanton and the cowboys, so my decision now was wait for him to come to town or try and hide out near Clanton's ranch and try and confront him when he left the bunch, if ever.

The ranch hadn't worked out so well and it was only pure luck and a woman wanting to escape that I was here. Likely that I was alive.

I decided to wait as it was said the cowboys were a Saturday night event in town, usually at The Charleston saloon and gambling house or the Oriental. No matter where I found him Mexican Bob was likely to be with a handful or more of the scum from Clanton's. So, my choice was, pick him off from some hideout and run from a murder warrant if found out, or face him and goad him into a fair fight. I had no interest in running from the law so the latter was my choice. Besides, I wanted to be close to watch the blood fill his lungs and the spark leave his eyes as he knew he was on the way to hell. Then again, should I prevail, he was worth at least a five-hundred-dollar bounty back in Wickenburg and Prescott.

My first stop was the bank where I drew out two hundred dollars. Then to the stage station to buy Elena a ticket to Johanson's. From there I went to The Grand and knocked gently on her door. I handed her the ticket and fifty dollars which would provide her with plenty for spending money along the way. The hug she gave me almost brought me to tears as it made me dwell on what I missed not celebrating my marriage to Sarah Ann. We parted with her "Via con Dios," ringing in my ears. I was not sure God was with me in my quest if you gave more weight to the admonition "turn the other cheek" than to "eye for eye."

I still had over fifty dollars in my pocket. Tipping generously, I was able to glean information from every bartender who wasn't too busy to gab. I was interested to learn the rivals in Tombstone were the Slopers, sporting men and gamblers mainly from California, most from San Francisco and the mining camps of the Sierra mountains and the Easterners, gamblers who had run the faro layouts and poker games in Kansas. Wichita, Dodge City, Ellsworth being the end of the great cattle drives where thousands changed hands at faro and poker tables. It was said the

Earps, prominent Easterners, were on their way to Tombstone to profit from the boom. Those with like backgrounds seem to attract one another, and alliances were formed, which led to conflicts. Thus, a man for breakfast every day.

It was Thursday, so if Saturday brought the cowboys to hurrah the town, I likely had two days to wait.

I found a grocer and bought a can of peaches for my lunch and a small can of lard, a bottle of Black Widow whiskey, and a box of .30 caliber cartridges for the Derringer. From there I went to the saddlery and looked at his collection of holsters and belts and fitted the Remington in a shoulder holster that hung under my left armpit. Only then did I retire to Farley's where we'd stabled the palomino and chestnut. The whiskey wasn't for me, but for the hostler Farley who was happy to receive and thus happy to let me spend some time behind his barn.

Greasing down the Colt's holster and the shoulder holster, I must have practiced my draw a hundred times with both. I also made sure the little .30 caliber Derringer was loaded and fit nicely in the left pocket of my light canvas coat.

Not to be outgunned I also greased both saddle scabbards so the coach gun and Sharps rode free and easy, should I require and live long enough to empty my handguns and get to them.

Of course I wanted to live, but watching Mexican Bob die hard was ahead of that wish.

As evening neared I decided to check the lay of the land and headed for The Charleston and the Oriental.

Chapter Thirty-Four

I left the Sharps with Farley for safekeeping but stuffed the coach gun in its scabbard and found space at the hitching rail outside the Oriental. With a town full of thieves and highbinders, you took a chance leaving anything tempting on your animals but then again, a thief took a bigger chance trying to steal a weapon or digging in a saddlebag that didn't belong to him. More than one thief had been sent to St. Peter when discovered with a hand in the wrong saddlebag.

I had gained some knowledge about the Occidental from reading the Epitaph, a week-old edition had this article:

LAST EVENING THE PORTALS WERE THROWN OPEN AND THE PUBLIC PERMITTED TO GAZE UPON THE MOST ELEGANTLY FURNISHED SALOON THIS SIDE OF THE GOLDEN GATE. TWENTY-EIGHT BURNERS SUSPENDED IN NEAT CHANDELIERS AFFORDED AN ILLUMINATION OF AMPLE BRILLIANCY AND THE BRIGHT RAYS REFLECTED FROM THE MANY COLORED CRYSTALS IN THE BAR SPARKLED LIKE A DECEMBER ICING IN THE SUNSHINE. THE SALOON COMPRISES TWO APARTMENTS. TO THE RIGHT OF THE MAIN ENTRANCE IS THE BAR, BEAUTIFULLY CARVED, FINISHED IN WHITE AND GILT AND CAPPED WITH A HANDSOMELY POLISHED TOP. IN THE REAR OF THIS STAND A BRACE OF SIDEBOARDS...THEY WERE MADE FOR THE BALDWIN HOTEL, OF SAN FRANCISCO...THE BACK APARTMENT IS COVERED WITH A BRILLIANT BODY BRUSSELS [SIC] CARPET AND SUITABLY FURNISHED AFTER THE STYLE OF A GRAND CLUB ROOM, WITH CONVENIENCES FOR THE WILY DEALERS IN POLISHED IVORY...TOMBSTONE HAS TAKEN THE LEAD AND [TO] MESSRS. JOYCE AND CO. OUR CONGRATULATIONS.

And the article didn't exaggerate. I'd never seen such opulence. That said, the customers were not nearly so well and expensively attired. Miners, draymen, cowhands, a few railroad workers, and even townsmen were well outclassed by silk, satin, and feather-clad soiled doves and bartenders and dealers in derbies, shirts with jet black studs, ties with diamond stickpins, and waistcoats with gold chains from watch to fob.

With my canvas trousers and coat, Lindsay Woolsey shirt, rough boots, black sombrero, and armory of weapons, I fit in with the former, not the latter. That said, every bartender sported a sidearm, every dealer a shoulder holster—he couldn't draw from a belt holster sitting down—and likely a knife in at least one pocket.

The Occidental was already crowded with hardly a space at the polished bar, so I wandered on to The Charleston. It was not the Occidental but was well appointed, and unlike the Occidental, among the customers was a table with four red-sash-clad cowboys. I was not disappointed to note none of them were those I'd crossed paths with at the Clanton ranch.

So, I quietly took a spot at the bar, one nearest the batwing doors in case I choose a quick exit. Nursing a beer, I stayed to myself and observed.

I'd sipped to the bottom of the mug and about

ready to head for Farley's and his haystack—I'd talked him into letting me bunk there with the bribe of the bottle of Black Widow—when four more sashed cowboys pushed through the batwings. Among them were the two who'd corralled me and dragged me to Old Man Clanton as well as the one I'd lollygagged with my Remington when making my escape from the house. They passed me without noticing and pulled up a table and chairs and joined the first four.

Not liking the odds I decided to make a graceful exit, but as fate would have it a dove walked up to take their order and the big old boy with the knot on his head looked up and locked eyes with me. I decided not to turn my back on them by escaping.

I could see him in serious conversation with the others, then he rose and elbowed through the crowd, shoved the miner near me out of the way, and gave me a hard stare which I returned in spades.

Finally, he growled, "You're the miserable whelp that blindsided me up at Clanton's."

As if in unison we both pulled our coats back to expose the revolvers at our sides. The astute bartender yelled to those behind him, "Clear out...trouble." And they filtered away.

I know he was surprised when rather than lay my hand on the butt of the Colt I held it away, but slipped my left into my coat pocket on that side.

I braced him. "I got no beef with you, big man. I was done wrong up at the Clanton's and just trying to flee the place...you were merely in the way."

"And you took off with Bob's woman."

"You Mexican Bob's protector or brother or what? She said she was her own woman and was kidnapped."

He was not swayed. "He's one of my pards, so I guess I'll have to kill you for all that."

My right hand was still far from my revolver when he went for his.

The first shot from the Derringer lit my coat on fire and took him between those worthless tits God gave man. His eyes went round as twenty-dollar gold pieces. His hands flew out, and he took a step back, then one hand grabbed the bar so he could keep his feet. The little .30 caliber probably killed him, but it would take him some time to die. He again reached for his revolver, and my second shot was aimed considerable higher and holed his Adam's apple, only then did I pat the fire out. He sunk to his knees, then fell forward on his face, his forehead resting on the toe of my left boot.

His cohorts at the table leaped up and started my way, revolvers in hand, as the customers between scattered like a covey of quail.

Before I could warn them, the bartender yelled and did so over the double barrel of a shotgun, "Set back down, boys. I'll send you one on the house. This was a fair fight and this youngster was only defending himself. I'll not have this beautiful place shot all to hell and gone."

They paused, looked at each other, then, obeying the double barrel, returned to their seats as a couple of other near customers put hands on knees and stared down at the fallen man.

To my surprise, one in a derby hat and waistcoat with woven silver threads shining, stood upright and pulled his coat back exposing a copper badge. "I'm Sheriff Behan. I'll need you to come over to the office and put your statement to writing...then I'd suggest you find a place to lay up where those gentlemen over at the table don't find you. I'll have your weapons."

With my revolver still in hand, with some

advantage over his holstered one, I said in a confident tone, "No, sir. You'll not pull my fangs while all those friends of this fella still have theirs."

He studied me a moment, then shrugged. "You'll walk in front of me. I'll not be back shot."

"I'll back out of here, then it's fine I lead the way."

Another well-dressed fellow stepped up. "Howdy, young man. I'm Forrest Swenny, newly elected mayor of Tombstone. I'll come along as I overheard and saw the whole affair." The mayor turned to Behan. "Self-defense, Johnny, if I ever saw it. You'll not be jailing this young fella, which I know you plan to do no matter your prevarications, as I'll not stain the town with a lynching."

The sheriff seemed displeased. He stepped forward and put a hard index finger in the mayor's chest. "Forrest, you'll not tell me how to enforce the law."

"So," the mayor replied in an even voice, "you want to come before the council again?"

Then Behan returned his gaze to me. "You'll not be jailed but you'll not leave town until you come before Judge Hollingsworth, and I'll know your whereabouts at all times. Understand?"

"Yes, sir. Let's ease out of here and I'll lead the

way." Then I turned to the mayor. "Appreciate you coming along, your honor."

"My pleasure, young man."

And we were off to the sheriff's office.

I was not surprised to glance back and see seven cowboys exit the Occidental and follow.

Chapter Thirty-Five

We were busy with a young fella taking my statement for over a half hour, with the mayor standing by. When finished, he sidled up to me. "I'll walk out with you, Mr. Callihan. Seems Spade Peabody's friends are across the street and awaiting your exit"—then he turned to Sheriff Behan—"or his jailing and you're handing him over to them after the good citizens of Tombstone have retired to their beds."

"Go to hell, Swenny," Behan said. "You have no proof I've ever violated my oath of office."

Sweeny replied, "I'll know where Mr. Callihan is at all times as it seems difficult to keep the workings of the sheriff's office private. Good enough for you?"

"You're the mayor, at least until the next election."

He turned to me. "Let's go."

We walked to the center of Allen Street and the mayor yelled at the seven on the front boardwalk of The Charleston, "Gentlemen, this is over for this day. Suggest y'all go inside and tell Horace the bartender the town is standing you all to two bottles of Who Hit John. I'll be along shortly to settle up. Mr. Callihan here will appear in front of Judge Hollingsworth in a day or two and you're all welcome to appear and give your version."

One of them yelled out, "If he lives that long."

But they all filtered into The Charleston. Only then did I fetch the chestnut and lead him as Sweeny walked me to Farley O'Tooles and cut me loose with my promise I'd be there in the hayloft or close by. A lie I easily told as I was sure the cowboys meant to make sure I was soon to meet my maker for outdrawing, actually thanks to Doc Holliday, outsmarting, one of their own.

As soon as Sweeny was out of sight, I crossed the road to a grocer, tied some salami, hard bread, cheese, pickles, a bottle of wine, and a half dozen sugar cookies in my coat and exited the back way. With scatter gun in one hand and groceries in the other, I strode down the alley to the rear of The

Grand, slipped in the back door, up the back stairs, and knocked quietly on Elena's door.

She was careful as I'd instructed. She didn't answer aloud, but I heard footfalls come near the door and advised her quietly. "Elena, it's Conn."

Quickly the door opened and I slipped inside and dropped the coat full of our supper on the bed. Again she threw her arms around me and hugged me until I near lost my breath. I pushed her away and held her, a hand on each shoulder.

"Seems they are hunting me as hard as they're hunting you. I know it's not proper, but no one knows I'm here and I need to make a nest on the floor over in that corner tonight. Then I'll walk you to the stage in the morning."

Again, she asked, "You can't come with me?"

"Not until my business with Mexican Bob is finished."

She locked eyes with me for a long moment, then sighed deeply. "Conn, you think Bob has been treating me properly. I'm no longer the girl you met at the post..." Her voice sunk an octave lower, and she dropped her eyes to the floor while she spoke, "If it pleases you, share the bed with me."

That took some breath away, like the hug she'd given me.

As tempted as I was, I sighed before I replied. "Elena, no matter what you say, that would be taking advantage in a way I was taught to fight shy of. As complimented as I am, I'd never believe you shared that bed with me out of anything but feeling a debt. When you're safe back with the Johanson's, and when you've had time to recover from the treatment of that thieving low life—and no one will ever know of what you just told me—you might see me coming up the trail."

She began to cry again.

I smiled. "How come it is I always make you cry?"

She just shook her head, then lay it on my chest. After a moment she pushed me away and laughed. "What's for supper, Conn Callihan. I'm famished."

Come morning there was enough bread and cheese left over for breakfast. I retired to the hotel restaurant and took my coffee while she got ready to go, by then it was time to walk to the stage station and send her off to the Johanson's on the nine o'clock.

We had to pass a half dozen saloons on the way, some of which had holdovers at the tables from the night before.

Approaching the Occidental, I noticed a

cowboy, plainly attired in his red sash, dozing on a bench out front. We crossed Allen Street with the hope of avoiding his gaze and I thought we were well past it when he jumped to his feet and disappeared inside at a run.

We'd just come even with Behan's office when I heard a yell and turned to see Mexican Bob swinging into the saddle and slipping a Winchester from its scabbard. I pushed Elena into the sheriff's office but Behan was exiting at the same time, and she rebounded back onto the boardwalk. So I spun and took four strides out into the dusty street.

I yelled back to the sheriff, "You'll want to pay close attention."

He yelled back, "Put down your weapons."

"Tell him that," I replied, motioning toward the oncoming rider.

Mexican was pounding our way at full gallop.

I guess the brave sheriff wanted nothing to do with a gun battle and he backed into his doorway out of sight.

Figuring Bob would pound on by, firing all the way, I dropped to one knee and shouldered the scattergun.

But he put the horse into a slide as he leaped

from the saddle. "You got my woman. Send her out and you can go on your way."

I'd used up my Doc Holliday belly gun in the pocket trick, so this looked like it was to be mano a mano.

So, I replied, "She tells me you're a low life murdering no account and the last thing she wants is more of your lying company."

He was fast, so fast he holed my coat before I could raise the shotgun. Holliday's words flashed by me, "it's not the fastest but the most accurate."

Turns out one doesn't have to be too damn accurate with a scatter gun at no more than twenty feet. One barrel I let go at the same time he got another shot off. Mine took him belly center and he flew back and landed with arms outstretched over his knees and extended like he was touching his toes. I heard one long sigh, like the air from my bellows at the forge, then he was quiet.

But it wasn't over, two cowboys ran from the Occidental, a revolver in each hand, firing as they came. Again, I remembered, accurate. I let them get to twenty feet distant and the second barrel of the coach gun, raised with one hand while I drew the revolver with the other, caught the leading cowboy mid-chest, and I raised my six-gun and pulled off carefully as hot lead creased my cheek. The second cowboy spun, firing both revolvers he held as he did. He dropped one as he hit the ground and tried to bring his weapon to bare again. I remembered another Holiday'ism, if one is good two is better, and the second shot put out his left eye and splattered the dust behind with blood and gore.

From behind, I heard that sweet voice I'd come to admire even more over the last couple of days. "You hurt, Conn?"

I took a moment to survey myself. One new hole in my canvas coat on the right side, two on the left, bleeding from the cheek but little more than had I been swiped at by a cactus. I didn't consider myself much to look at so a scar on the cheek seemed to matter little.

Surveying the street I could see that half the town was out on the boardwalks, and a half dozen reached me the same time Behan did.

He held a Winchester and snapped at me, "Give me your weapons."

I was gratified when a half dozen town folks, led by my new friend Farley O'Toole, chimed in. "Self-defense, Behan, we all saw it."

I glanced at Behan. "I'll be back to give a statement, Sheriff, soon as I walk this lady to the stage."

Again, the crowd confirmed my innocence and surrounded the sheriff so he couldn't interfere with my safely delivering her, as Elena and I strolled toward the station.

Only then, as we walked along, did I realize my quest was over. Nine men I owed, and who owed Sarah Ann, one who got in the way, and two more who decided to fill me full of lead for finishing my task.

Like it or not, Conn Callihan was now a man with a reputation.

There was no reason I couldn't accompany Elena, except I need to stay and make sure my name was clear and there'd be no flyers out with my likeness.

I also realized I'd have another reward coming back in Wickenburg.

This collecting bounty money was getting to be a habit.

Maybe I'd take it up for a living.

If inventory was the necessity of a successful business, and those with flyers on them the inventory of a bounty hunter, then the proverbial shelves of the territories were flush with inventory to profit from.

Arizona territory alone was a cornucopia of goods.

Afterword

I'd decided Tombstone not a healthy place for an aspiring bounty hunter even if half the cowboys in town had flyers out on them. The problem was staying alive to haul them to the law. I was reloading the chestnut's saddle bags, thinking I would make a slow easy ride back to Prescott where I'd enjoy returning Sarah Ann's twenty-five hundred dowry to old man Macintosh and maybe organize a few fellas to mine a cave I was sure would be a payday...when a pair of wagons rolled into town.

Virgil Earp held the reins of one, Wyatt Earp the other. And it looked like they came to stay a good while as family was in tow.

I tipped my hat to Virgil as he passed, and it seemed he recognized me.

The rumor was Doc Holliday was wrapping up business in Prescott and would soon join them.

Soon I was disappointed to hear Wyatt had no intention of putting on a badge, but rather planned to mine the miners at a faro game should he find one that would take him on as dealer, he also planned to do some prospecting.

Virgil, on the other hand, quickly wore the badge of deputy marshal, even before I could welcome him to town.

I had new hope the town would gain respectability as had so many under the hawk eye of the Earp's. I might be able to stay on and maybe put some of my newfound riches to work, maybe a forge or who knows what.

One thing I knew for sure, I'd make friends with the Earp's and gain their confidence.

If all I'd heard was true, they were men to ride the river with.

A Look At
Callihan: The Earps

From the author of *Callihan: Valley of Skulls* comes *Callihan: The Earps*, a thrilling YA Western packed with grit, justice, and unbreakable bonds.

Conn Callihan thought vengeance would end his troubles, but the silver boom town of Tombstone had other plans. Fresh from avenging the brutal murder of his young bride, Conn's deadly reputation as a shootist and bounty hunter followed him like a shadow.

But Conn isn't riding this trail alone. With the unlikely friendship of the Earps and Doc Holliday, Conn tries to carve out a life worth living—even as he becomes the guardian of three orphans, two ripped away by an Apache raid. As he battles to bring them home, the threats multiply. Ike Clanton and his cowboys want Conn out of the way, and the Dragoon Mountains hold dangers that could break even the toughest soul.

Survival in Tombstone means more than just holding your ground. Can Conn protect his adopted family and stand his ground against every enemy, or will the dust of the frontier finally claim him?

AVAILABLE JANUARY 2025

About the Author

L. J. Martin is the author of 70 young adult, classic western, historical and thriller novels with a half-dozen non-fiction works among the mix. His first novel was a Y.A. and is still in print. As the father of four boys he was adamant about them filling their days with good books, books that taught values and how great the American experience is and was. He lives in Montana on a small ranch and winters in Prescott, Arizona, both homes in western areas steeped in history. Having wrangled, packed mules, farmed and ranched, sailed his own ketch, and studied history all his life, he's particularly suited to writing about what he loves, the west. He's lived among and studied its critters, ranchers, miners, soldiers, mariners, river men and townsmen and women, and their history. His most recent historical endeavor was writing/directing/producing the classic western film EYE FOR EYE, adapted from his novella of the same name. Please visit his webpage http://www.ljmartin.com.